D1580411

The Final Test

The Final Test

by

GARETH OWEN

Illustrated by Paul Wright

LONDON
VICTOR GOLLANCZ LTD
1985

First published in Great Britain 1985
by Victor Gollancz Ltd,
14 Henrietta Street, London WC2E 8QJ

© Gareth Owen 1985
Illustrations © Paul Wright 1985

British Library Cataloguing in Publication Data
Owen, Gareth
  The final test.
  I. Title
  823'.914[J]   PZ7

ISBN 0-575-03699-0

Typeset in Great Britain by Centracet
and printed by St Edmundsbury Press,
Bury St Edmunds, Suffolk

*This novel is dedicated to Pauline Woodhead
and her class at Watermill Primary School,
Selly Oak, Birmingham, without whom it would
never have been written.*

Chapter One

Looking back to that summer holiday in 1947 it seems to me that the sun was always shining and the days went on for ever. I suppose it all started with the tennis ball. In those days they were precious and I never went anywhere without one. Once you somehow managed to get hold of one you hung on to it as though your life depended on it. I can remember now how during a long and seemingly never ending lesson I would slip my hand into my jacket pocket just to check it was still there. It may sound strange but I sometimes even dreamed of finding four or five brand new ones all together in a nest of long grass by the dirty thatched cottage in Pinfold Lane. A kind of golden hoard, an Eldorado of tennis balls, enough to keep me supplied right through the football and the cricket season. All through the autumn and winter there'd be a ball at my feet, dribbling along the pavements and crashing in shots against front gates. In the summer I'd be flinging it so that it ricocheted off garden walls for me to perform miraculous catches in the slips. And I invented the rules. The quarter of a mile I travelled from school to home each day was a minefield. The ball had to be dribbled on the pavement and never run into the road. At each gate I had to drive the ball past some imaginary goalkeeper and then trap the rebound. If I missed the gate I had to go back two. If I failed to trap the ball I had to go back three. If it went into a garden I had to go right back to the beginning again; and so it went on. I sometimes wonder how I ever managed to get home at all. While all this was going on, I'd be pouring out an hysterical commentary, complete with crowd noises, in which my miraculous skill with the ball was fulsomely praised. To any passer-by I was a ten-year-old boy kicking a scuffed tennis ball aimlessly about the place, but in my head I was an England star going for glory.

On this particular afternoon, as it was summer, I was playing the cricket variation of the game. It was that best time of all. The last Friday of the summer term. School was over for long enough to make it seem like for ever and the real holiday didn't start until the following Monday. It was all ahead. Six weeks of holiday stretched out in front of me like a sunlit and untrodden road where anything was possible and anything could happen. By the age of ten I'd already found out that looking forward to something was often far better than what happened. And there were always definite things to look forward to, like my trial for the County Under Eleven team at the beginning of August. If I managed to get into that team there'd be the inter-County knockout competition and then the chance of the late tour of Devon and Cornwall in September with three extra weeks off school. That would make nine weeks of holiday. That's why it was important to keep practising. So bang went the ball against the wall. Good length, just a touch of spin. And back it came into my waiting hand. "And a brilliant caught and bowled by Tattershall." Yes, it was going to be a wonderful summer.

There was only one blot on the horizon, and that was the long, white envelope in my jacket pocket. My school report. I knew there were far too many "Talks more than he works" and "Must learn to take more care" in Miss Lovejoy's thin, spidery handwriting to please my father. And me being twenty-third out of a class of twenty-six wasn't going to make him hop about with joy either. For a second I thought of losing it, accidentally on purpose. I'd put on a worried look and say, "Dad, they're not giving out reports this year. Paper shortage because of the War. Shame really, Dad, I would have got a really good one." Be no good though. Dad would only have to ring up and then I'd be in double trouble. First for telling lies and second for having a bad report. Big Sawbridge cycled past the top of the road with a couple of his mates. I half hoped he'd see me, come over, bash my nose and pinch my report. Then I'd have blood on me as proof. But they didn't see me and cycled round the corner, whistling. Maybe it wouldn't be so bad. If I could catch this bounce off number forty-three there'd be enough good remarks to satisfy him. I was always making bargains like that with myself. The ball spun back viciously but I managed to catch it. "If I can hit the Leamington Avenue road sign and catch the ball before the grid, I'll get a place in the County Under Eleven team." I fumbled the ball but just managed to catch it before it hit the road. Things might be all right.

To be on the safe side I decided to take the long way, past the big posh houses in Sanford Avenue, instead of the short cut through Halifax Road. Dad had a meeting that night after tea so if I was a bit late he'd have gone out again and I'd be in bed by the time he got back. It was worth a try. The walls in Sanford Avenue were low, not more than a foot high, topped by tall privet hedges. You could never see the houses because of the laburnums, rhododendrons and tall trees that lay beyond. This was a tough wall to bounce my off breaks against because unless I was really accurate there was a good chance of me losing my tennis ball. But on this day I felt that nothing could go wrong. In my imagination I saw the batsman taking guard. There was a spot on the pitch, in reality a crack in the pavement. The delivery was fine. It hit the crack perfectly but then leapt crazily over that low wall and into the jungle of bushes. There were no gates on this side and to go round by the front meant being in full view of the houses. Apart from that I knew quite a lot of the owners kept savage dogs. "Plenty to lose in those houses," my mother used to say. Dogs or no dogs, there was nothing for it. I took a quick look both ways and stepped over the low wall. The bushes were much thicker than I had imagined. It was more like a wood than a garden. Branches brushed against my face, cutting out the sunlight. I walked carefully, searching the ground. There was no sight of the ball. It must have gone further in. I walked deeper into the wood, scuffing with my feet. A branch tore at my face drawing blood. A pigeon, disturbed by my presence, crashed up through the branches, making me jump. The trees seemed to go on for ever; what I had thought was a collection of bushes was a dense wood. I decided that the ball couldn't possibly have come this far and turned back in the direction of the road. But the wall didn't appear. This was daft. I couldn't be lost, not a few yards from the road. As I was beginning to panic I saw light and a break in the trees.

I pushed through the last few trees, looking down for the wall. But there was no wall there. At first I couldn't understand. I was sure the wall ran the full length of the road. Then I lifted my gaze. I was standing on a raised

10

bank of grass that ran down to a neatly cropped lawn. The bank ran round the lawn, sloping down like an amphitheatre. I had come in completely the wrong direction. On the side furthest away from me was a raised smaller area of lawn and behind that a cluster of buildings that made up the house. There was a raised wooden verandah running along the front and over the windows were clean red and white awnings. And near a garden seat lay the dog. He was the biggest dog I'd ever seen. At first I thought he was asleep but he raised his head and looked at me. Sleepily he pulled himself to his feet and trotted inquisitively towards me.

His tail wasn't wagging and there was a dangerous look in his eyes. I retreated a few yards back into the woods, but slowly so as not to startle him. I remember reading somewhere that you never show a dog that you're frightened. I kept my eyes fixed on him. He returned my gaze. Under my breath I was saying to myself, "If he doesn't attack me, I'll leave the ball and go straight home with my report," when something else caught my eye. My tennis ball. There it was, nestling beneath the seat. It couldn't have bounced that far. The dog must have picked it up and carried it. The dog! As I had disappeared into the edge of the wood the dog had lost interest and returned to the shelter of the garden seat. He picked up the ball in his jaws, looked round for a second then dropped it between his enormous paws. Slowly his head dropped and he fell asleep. A bee buzzed noisily amongst some petals. I held my breath. I'd never been brave about dogs, not since I'd been bitten on the arm by Mrs Poole's husky. I still had the scar high up on my arm where his teeth had torn at me. John Eccles had nearly had his ear taken off by an Alsatian on the Sunday School trip to

11

Morecambe. He said you didn't feel pain because of the shock. Just your face turning wet with the blood. I let my breath out slowly and quietly. I had to have that ball. I was striking another bargain with myself. "If you don't fetch that ball, it'll rain on the day of the County trial and you'll never get another chance." I closed my eyes for a second and breathed in, then tip-toed across the lawn. It seemed to go on for ever. The closer I got the bigger the dog became. His jaws were half open and his great tongue lolled out like a carpet over a set of very sharp-looking teeth. I decided to approach him from behind.

I made a slight detour, mounting the slope to the smaller lawn before the house, about ten yards to the dog's right. I dropped on my hands and knees and crawled forwards almost an inch at a time. I was nearly there when he turned over with a growl. I almost turned to run but he fell asleep again with a sigh. More than anything I wished I could have been at home having tea. The ball was touching his fur. I wondered if he could smell me. Was I down wind? I crouched lower and edged closer and closer, scarcely daring to breath. My heart thundered in my ears and there was sweat running down my forehead. The place was alive with the song of birds and from the house came the sound of a woman singing and a baby gurgling with laughter. You could almost have been in the depths of the country. I stretched my fingers out towards the ball. Closer and closer. My fingers touched it, clasped it. It was in my hand. Then suddenly I was on my back on the ground. The dog had jerked awake and was standing over me, his muzzle almost on my face. I could feel his breath. I closed my eyes in terror. My face. It was wet. Just like Eccles had said. There was no pain, no pain at all. Just the blood. Slowly I opened my eyes.

14

The dog's great tongue was licking my nose with urgent persistence.

"Good dog," I whispered and tickled his ears. He seemed to laugh at that, then suddenly rolled over on his back and rolled joyfully from side to side. I had made a friend. I couldn't hang about though. Somebody might come out of the house at any moment. Giving the dog a last pat I descended to the lawn. It was then I noticed something I hadn't seen before. Well, seen, but you know how it's possible to look sometimes and not see something that's right under your nose. That's what had happened to me. Probably because I was concentrating so hard on the ball and the dog. What I saw on that beautifully cut lawn was a row of miniature men, all about as tall as a man's hand from the wrist to the tip of the finger. They had been expertly cut and modelled from plywood and each one was dressed in white cricket gear and wore a cap. At either end was a white sight screen and on the boundary nearest the wood a miniature score-board which said:

AUSTRALIA	150
WICKETS	2
LAST MAN	43

In the exact centre of the lawn the two creases were marked out neatly in white paint and there were two sets of cricket stumps complete with bails. It was like something frozen in time. Like that story Miss Lovejoy told us once about the *Marie Celeste*. A boat abandoned in the middle of the ocean. All the places laid for dinner. Nothing out of place, not a soul in sight. It was just like that. I wondered if I was dreaming, but when you're

15

asleep you don't know if you're awake and when you are awake you're absolutely certain you're not dreaming. I half expected a couple of Australian batsmen to emerge from the shadow of the verandah to continue the innings while the spectators clapped. I half closed my eyes. The fielders looked so real. At one end was a bat, complete in every detail. The handle had been carefully bound with cotton. There was even a signature on the blade just like on a real cricket bat. I picked it up. It read, 'Alan Kippax'. I wondered who he was. Beside the bat lay a marble. Obviously the ball. I couldn't resist it. I picked up the marble between finger and thumb and kneeling down I bowled it at the wicket which was about a stride and a half away. It missed. There was skill in this game and it obviously required two players. I bent to pick up the marble.

"You should really open with Larwood," said a voice from over to my left. Slowly I turned round.

Chapter Two

I've never been very good at facing up to things. I'm not
a coward but if I can avoid a fight, I will. So when I
heard this voice, my first thought was to make a dash for
it into the woods. But, you know, something stronger
than fear made me hesitate. It was curiosity. Curiosity is
one of my great faults. I'm really nosey about everything.
I can't help it. That's probably why I keep getting into
trouble all the time. I remember my dad reading me a
story once when I was about five. It was all about this cat
and all he did was go around asking questions and
sticking his nose into everything. Like he'd see a parcel or
something and he'd say, "'Scuse me what's in the parcel?"
Always said "'Scuse me." I thought that was dead good.
"'Scuse me" all over the place. My dad told me he read
that story because he knew I was like the cat. I think he
was right. Now, the thing I was curious about at that
particular moment, was those miniature cricketers on the
lawn. So I turned round to see where the voice was
coming from.

At first I couldn't see anything too clearly because the
trees were casting long dark shadows but then I saw a
kind of cane chair with an extra bit at the front to support
your legs. It had big wheels on either side and was a bit
like the chair that the old grandpa sits in who gives Lord
Snooty fivers for pushing him down to the sea. An

invalid's chair with a red blanket on it. As far as I could see, though, there was nobody on the chair and I thought, "Hello I'm having an hallucination." Then the blanket moved and a pale hand sort of floated up and waved me over. "Must be an old grandad," I thought to myself. I looked round. There was nobody else in sight. There wasn't much danger. If it was just an old man in a wheelchair I could soon outrun him. Even if he was the champion wheelchair driver of all time he'd never catch me going through those trees. I wandered over and stood in front of the chair. The blanket moved and I got a real shock. Well, two shocks really. Shock number one was that the face that came into view wasn't old at all but belonged to a boy of about my own age. That shook me a bit because I immediately thought, "is he going to be able to run as fast as me?" The second shock was that he was really pale and his eyes looked enormous because his face was so thin. His hair was a sort of yellowy-gold and hung down over his forehead. Altogether he looked like somebody who'd been locked up in a dark room where there wasn't a barber. So there were two things to be nosey about. One, the cricket and two, why had he spent his whole life locked up in a dark room where they didn't believe in haircuts?

Now it's all right for a cat in a story to ask questions straight out, but for people it's different. It is for me anyway. I always have to go round about. My dad says I couldn't walk in a straight line if I wanted to. For instance, I don't seem to be able to go through a front gate. If there's a big front gate, wide open and welcoming, and somebody is standing there smiling and waving me in, what do I do? I go all the way round the back and crawl through the hedge. It's my character. So for a moment I stood there, embarrassed, staring round at the trees, pretending there was something really interesting going on that was catching my attention. He was obviously feeling the same. Dead embarrassed. I often get like that when I'm talking to one person. In a crowd it's fine. You can get lost in all the remarks and laughs. You can make really stupid remarks but nobody really notices. The worst is when you meet a teacher out of school on your own. I never know what to say. My voice goes all funny and I keep pulling daft faces all over the place. Well, this was how I felt with this kid. I could understand why he wasn't saying anything. It must be a bit frightening if you've been locked up in the dark for years and a complete stranger comes wandering in. I knew how he felt. What happened next was what always happens. You start making stupid remarks. Just saying anything at all so long as there's no silence. What happens of course is that none of the remarks have anything to do with what went before. So the conversation was:

"I came for my ball." Well, that was really stupid to start with. I mean he must have seen me come in. What did he think I'd come for? To kill a rhinoceros?

Then he said, "The dog's asleep."

"I thought you was a grandad."

"He doesn't bite."

"Is this your house?"

"Have some orange."

"I got bitten once."

"Do you play cricket?"

"Is this your house?"

I'm not going to tell you the rest because it went on for about five minutes like this. Then I suddenly said, "Yes please." He looked a bit surprised. The reason he looked a bit surprised was because he'd just said, "How old are you?"

It just doesn't make sense to say, "Yes please," in answer to "How old are you?" But I was still talking about the orange juice. I gave a cough.

"Orange juice," I explained, "I'd like some orange juice."

He picked up a jug that was on a small table. Next to it were some green pills in a bottle and some dark-coloured medicine. It wasn't like the orange juice we had at home, that Mum bought off the Corona man, but really nice. Like real oranges with bits floating about in it. I drank the whole glass to pass the time. All the while he watched me with this kind of calm smile on his face. He didn't twitch about like most kids would but just watched me. When I gave him the empty glass back he put it on the table and then asked me the question I always dread being asked. He asked me my name. When anybody asks my name I get really embarrassed. Teachers can never understand what I'm saying the first time so I always have to say it a few times, every time louder than the time before. So, by the time they can understand, the whole class is laughing and sniggering and I'm going redder and redder. Well my second name is Tattershall, which is fine, but my first name is Cecil. I really hate it. How could anybody be so stupid as to give me that name. Cecil! It must be the most stupid name in the universe. Anybody who calls their son Cecil should be dropped off a high building into a lake of boiling custard. It wouldn't be so bad being called Cecil as long as I had another name. But no. It was just Cecil. What the kids at school call me is Taters. Taters so that it rhymes with 'waiters'. I don't like Taters very much but it's a million times better than Cecil. Anything is better than Cecil.

"Taters," I said.

Well I meant to say "Taters" but for some reason what came out was "Cecil". I could have kicked myself. But then an amazing thing happened. Or rather, didn't happen. He didn't laugh. Didn't even smile. He was the first kid in the whole world who hadn't laughed at my name. There and then I knew that this pale-faced boy with the long hair was really something out of the ordinary. Anybody who doesn't laugh at the name Cecil has got to be special, haven't they? Right away all my embarrassment disappeared and we started talking together as if we'd known each other all our lives.

He told me his name was Skipper and that he'd changed it from Skipton, just like I'd done. Then when I told him that I'd thought he was a grandad he laughed so much he nearly fell off his chair.

"I'm an invalid," he said, waving at the bottles and the pills. "We used to live in India but I got this disease so my father and mother rented this house because the climate was supposed to be beneficial. I have a bad chest too," he explained. Nobody I knew would use the word "beneficial" because all the kids would have laughed but it just came naturally out of Skipper. There was no showing off.

"Don't you go to school?" I asked.

"I've never been to school. I have a private tutor."

"Some people have all the luck," I said.

He beckoned me forward. "Would you like to listen to my chest?" he asked. "It makes some jolly decent noises." Skipper could always think of interesting things to do.

He pulled back the red blanket and opened his blue and

22

white pyjamas. His skin was the colour of paper. I put my ear to his chest. I'd never listened to anybody's chest before. Strange wheezings and creakings filled my head. When he breathed in and out it sounded like somebody playing a broken church organ at the bottom of a swimming-pool.

"Good noises aren't they?"

"Dead good," I said.

"They used to be louder," he said, "but I'm getting better." He sounded disappointed. I was really jealous of those noises. I had nothing to compare with that. I sometimes get athlete's foot where all the bits between your toes go mushy and smell horrible but I had a feeling he wouldn't like to have that shoved under his nose. I had to think of something.

"My stomach rumbles sometimes," I offered feebly. "You know, gurgles and so on."

"Very good," he said.

I don't think he was really impressed. He was just being polite.

"Sometimes in bed at night," I went on, "it sounds like voices. I can almost understand what they're saying."

He smiled and nodded. There was a pause while he took a pill and washed it down with orange juice. He put the glass down.

"I nearly died once," he said flatly.

That was the thing about Skipper. He was always coming out with something right out of the blue that was dead interesting. I sat down on the grass next to him.

"What did it feel like?" I asked.

He frowned for a minute. "Mostly like going to sleep. I felt very tired and when I woke up there were a lot of nurses and doctors looking down at me."

"Did you see any angels or anything?"

He thought about that a bit. "No, no angels."

"Music?"

"No."

I picked a blade of grass and chewed it. I'd never been dead. Never even been ill. Except for the dog bite and the chicken-pox I'd got three years before. My mum got it as well but she kept on nursing me. Then I thought of something.

"My Granny died once," I said. "I heard my mum and dad talking about it when I was in bed one night. They said she heard music. But the wireless was on."

"Wonder what it's like to be dead," Skipper said.

"Must be like before you're born."

Skipper looked at me and nodded.

Later on I found that with Skipper I could think of things that had never come into my head before, or maybe they were there but he made them come out. I tried to put on my intelligent face. You know, when you frown a lot as if you're thinking of something very deep. While I was doing my intelligent look I suddenly remembered the cricketers on the lawn. I thought I'd better bring the conversation round slowly. So I started telling him how I was going to have a trial for the County. He was really interested in that and asked me all sorts of questions.

"Perhaps by the time you play I'll be better enough to come and see you," he said.

His father had played a few games for Yorkshire before the War as a guest amateur. Skip said he'd always wanted to be a professional cricketer himself but he'd never been well enough. This was the moment, I thought.

"Is that why you play the miniature game?" I asked trying to sound casual.

"You've been dying to ask me that, haven't you?"

He seemed to know what was going on in my mind. He asked me to pick up a couple of the fielders. When I gave them to him he held them in both hands as though they were precious.

"Father made them. They're all meant to be somebody." He put one of them in my hand. It was slightly shorter than the other. The sleeves were rolled up above the elbows and the short hair was brown and brushed back.

"He's very special," explained Skipper. "He's Larwood!"

That was the name he'd said to me earlier. "Bring on Larwood," he'd said. I'd never heard of him.

"He played before the War. Fast bowler. He was so fast he frightened the Australians. He was the fastest bowler there's ever been. My father played against him once. He said he was so fast that when you just stopped the ball the bat shook in your hands. This is Jardine," he said holding up the other man. "He was the captain."

Jardine had a thin, unhappy face with a long nose. Again, Skipper seemed to read what was in my mind.

"He wants to beat the Australians so badly that it makes him look unhappy. There's no point playing unless you want to win. Otherwise it just becomes a game." He looked up towards the trees and picked at a thread on his blanket. There was a silence.

"Don't you play now?" I asked.

"No," said Skip. "Not any more." His face was sad. I won't ask him, I thought to myself.

"Dad and me, we were replaying the 1932–33 Tests.

25

Every time he came home on leave we'd play another Test. They'd each last three days."

"But you didn't finish this one."

A shadow fell across Skipper's face. I shivered. It was getting cold.

"No, never finished," he said. "We'd just started this game when Dad was called back to his ship. He was the captain of a frigate." Skip shrugged his shoulders. "He didn't come back."

"What happened?" I asked.

"His ship was escorting a convoy when a submarine torpedo hit them. They were all killed."

My dad hadn't even joined the army. He'd been knocked over by a bike ridden by a baker's boy when he was fourteen and hurt his back so the War Office had turned him down. It wasn't his fault. Quite a few kids at school had had their dads killed during the War. When this happened our headmaster, Mr Quinney, had them come out the front and told everybody in assembly about it. Some of the kids cried but some of them, especially the boys, held their heads up like you're supposed to do when you're being brave. I was dead jealous. But not one of them had ever had a. dad who'd died while he was captain of a frigate. Some kids have all the luck.

I began telling Skip how my dad had been run over by a tank in the trenches, but, just as I was starting, I saw this look in his eye and I knew straight off that he'd see I was lying. So I told the truth. He didn't laugh or anything. I felt I could say anything to Skipper. He looked over the pitch. Shadows were beginning to stretch across it.

"So it's always stayed like that . . ."

"Like the . . ."

"*Marie Celeste*," we both said together and laughed.

26

Skipper wheeled the chair down the slope. I suddenly noticed how thick his arms were. He could really move those wheels. He leant over the side and picked up another player. It wasn't as well made as the others.

"This one's Dad," he said. "I made it afterwards." He put it back in its position on the long leg boundary. "Since I've been out of bed I sit up there and pretend it's real."

"I did that," I said. "I imagined the not-out batsmen coming out." I made the noise of a crowd applauding with my mouth.

"McCabe and Bradman," said Skipper.

I'd never heard of McCabe. "That's right," I said.

"I'm going to see Bradman next summer when the Australians come over."

"I do that at home too," I said. "You know, pretend things are real." I'd never admitted this to anybody before, not even John Eccles, in case they thought I was daft. "I've never told this to anyone before in case they thought I was daft," I said.

"Do you look at pictures?"

"Yes," I said.

"Screw your eyes up?"

"I do that."

"Me as well."

I wondered if I could risk telling him about the picture at home.

"We have this picture. My dad stuck it on my bedroom wall. Lots of fighting in the olden days. When it's half dark you screw your eyes up and it looks as if they're moving."

"Me too."

"Dead good."

27

"Yeah, dead good."

There was a pause.

I said, "Do you do escapes?"

"Escapes?"

"Well, when I'm in bed or in class sometimes, I imagine I'm little. Dead small. Like about the size of my thumb. It's me but I can sort of watch myself at the same time. And I'm on the curtains and I work out how I get down crawling along the curtain rail, then down the curtains with little ropes and ladders. In class, by the time I've escaped the bell's usually gone."

"I do that too," said Skip.

"Never."

"I do, honest."

It was amazing that he should think the same things as me. Up until that moment I thought I was the only one in the whole world who did escapes. I thought of something else.

"We do toenails at school."

"Toenails?" he said. He didn't know about toenails. I could tell by the look on his face.

"Me and John Eccles and Barry Cross. It's like stupid French, you know. Like the teacher will say we have to do a test so we change all the words to toenails. The teacher says, 'Put your hands up.' And we say, 'Put your toenails up.' That kind of thing. Or if she tells us to write in our best handwriting, we say 'I want you to write in your best toenails.' Sometimes we say, 'Toenails esty grand.'"

He hadn't heard of toenails.

"Toenails esty grand. It's just something we say. It's funny."

He swigged down one of his green pills. It must have tasted bad because he shivered.

"Tastes horrible?" I said.

"Toenails," he said. He was very quick at catching on, was Skip.

Our talking was really quick now. We kept saying all these things that we did that were the same. You know how sometimes you're having a conversation with somebody and there are long silences while you try and think of something to say, and you're whistling and coughing and shuffling your feet trying to show you're not embarrassed when all the time you are. And, with me, my eyebrows go shooting up and down. Well none of that happened with Skip. And I could feel my eyebrows being dead still and normal. We could hardly wait for the other to stop talking before butting in. I couldn't believe it.

Eventually I plucked up the courage to ask him what I'd been dying to say all afternoon. I nodded towards the players.

"D'you think we could play?"

Skipper looked at me. I noticed one of his eyes was a different colour from the other. One blue and one a sort of hazel.

He said, "I shouldn't really. Because if I go on with the game . . ." He stopped.

"It'll mean your dad's not coming back."

I don't know where that came from. I just thought it and it popped out. Skipper looked at me for a long time before speaking.

"Yes," he said, "I suppose so."

I was disappointed that I wouldn't be able to play but I could understand.

It was getting really dark. I was going to be in dead trouble off my mum when I got home. I got up to leave.

"On the other hand," said Skipper, "maybe he'd like the game to go on." He looked up into the sky. It was up to him to decide. I wasn't going to say anything, even though I really wanted to have a go.

"Dad hated leaving anything unfinished."

His face didn't look as pale as before. More a golden colour or perhaps it was the light.

"Can you push me over and help me out?" he said.

Once I'd got him down the slope he was all right. He sort of let himself fall out of the chair but he was really agile. I could see his legs didn't work too well. The right one he had to move with his hands. He settled down, sort of half lying behind the wicket.

"You have to hold the bat at the top with only your finger and thumb so all your fingers are pointing straight down." The cigar box that he used as a wicket keeper was at an angle underneath his chin.

"You bowl," he said, looking round the field just like a real batsman. "You have to kneel up."

I did what he told me. The first ball was wrong.

"It has to be underhand. Just let it roll out of your hand from up by your chest. Otherwise it's too easy."

I held the marble between finger and thumb and lobbed it with a bit of spin on to what I thought was a good length. Skipper hooked it for six.

"Better you fetch it," said Skipper. He pointed down. "No good, these rotten old legs."

I fetched the ball back from the boundary. I went to adjust the score-board.

"This isn't a real game," he said, "just a practice." I adjusted the field a little.

"Play," I shouted. This ball was better but Skipper leaned back and square cut it to the off boundary in front of the house. It was then I saw her. A tall woman with a baby in her arms. She ignored me and spoke sharply to Skipper.

"Malcolm, what in heaven's name are you doing? Get up this instant. That grass is damp and you only got up the day before yesterday."

His mum, I thought. Malcolm must be his name. She looked really cross. She walked across to the wheelchair and wheeled it to where Skip was crouched. She had on a white dress and brown and white shoes. As she went by I could smell her perfume.

"I've told you about this," she said. "You know what the doctor said about the damp at this time of the afternoon."

"This is Taters," said Skipper as he struggled into the chair. "I was just showing him how to play."

"Taters?" said his mother. She had a funny sort of accent. Not posh, just different.

"Taters," explained Skipper; "rhymes with waiters."

"Well that's all very well," she said, "but I think it's about time you went home. Your mother will be wondering where you've got to." She wheeled Skipper over to where I was standing.

"Does your mother know where you are?" she asked. She sounded firm but at the same time not unkind.

"Sort of," I said shrugging my shoulders.

"Sort of," she repeated with a smile. The baby woke up and began to laugh then changed the laugh into a yawn.

I gave the marble to Skip and started to trudge off. "Well, I'll be off," I said.

I could hear them whispering. I had just reached the wood when I heard Skip shout, "Taters."

I turned round.

His mother had her arm round his shoulders.

"Why not come over tomorrow?"

"If you want to," said his mother. She was smiling and serious at the same time.

I gave a wave. "Thanks," I said.

"After lunch," said Skipper's mum.

"When's that?" I asked.

"About two," she said.

I nodded and gave a wave. Not a proper big wave but the little one I'd been practising. Low near the hip. I don't think they noticed it. In the depths of the wood I heard Skipper shout.

"Hey," he said.

"Hey," I repeated. I couldn't see him now.

"Toenails," I heard his voice say.

"Esty grand," I shouted back, and then I was over the wall.

That night I lay staring at the ceiling watching this daddy-long-legs but my mind was somewhere else. I was coming down to a beautiful lawn. There were miniature people all round and at one end was a stand. On the field miniature cricketers were playing. The batsman at one end lifted the ball into the air. He had very strong arms but his legs didn't look right. The ball flew over the pavilion and I caught it. Suddenly a man in a naval cap appeared over the opposite side of the field. There were flames all over his face. He stretched out his hand. He seemed to want the marble. I shook my head. My mouth was saying, "No, no." But no words were coming out. I woke up with a jolt. Downstairs I could hear my mum and dad talking.

"What shall we do with him?" my dad was saying.

It was my report. I fell asleep.

Chapter Three

"The sun is shining brilliantly this morning here at Sydney as Larwood, fastest and most feared of bowlers, comes running in to bowl. What a beautiful action. Up goes the left arm, down goes that left foot and the right arm flashes over. It's short and whistles past the left ear of Woodfull, the Australian opener."

The marble pounded against the metal cigar-box wicket keeper and out towards square leg. I scampered after it and lobbed it back to Skipper. A sparrow hopped in front of the score-board and the July sun was warm on my back. The First Test had started. On the smaller lawn before the house Skipper's mother sipped a glass of lemon tea as she watched us. Baby Sophie slept in her pram.

"Keep the bat straight," shouted Skipper. "It's just like real cricket, keep the bat straight."

I patted the crease. Skipper moved Jardine in just a little closer. Just on a good length was a worn patch. If Larwood dropped it there I would be in real trouble. Skipper knelt up and brushed the hair out of his eyes. His hand was above his shirt pocket. For fast bowling you couldn't swing your arm. It all had to be done with the wrist. But it was still fast. The trouble with Larwood was that he was not only the fastest bowler alive but also the most accurate.

"Play," said Skipper. I faced up. Skip continued the commentary.

"And it's Larwood again. Really getting up speed here. Bowls it short just outside the off stump and Woodfull cracks it away to the off boundary. Four runs."

"Beautiful square cut," I added. I was proud of that shot.

"You're getting the idea," said Skipper.

But Larwood's next ball hit the spot, caught the shoulder of the bat, and struck the cigar box without bouncing. Caught behind.

Even as he hopped down the wicket, his legs dragging behind him, Skipper was commentating.

"And that's the bare patch that Larwood has been aiming for. I don't think many people saw that ball, it was so fast. Woodfull, the Australian opener, certainly didn't and it thumped into the wicket keeper's gloves."

It was my turn to bowl.

We'd started at two o'clock that afternoon. When I had arrived through the wood (I couldn't bring myself to use the front way) Skipper was driving his wheelchair up and down alongside the wicket, watering it from a watering-can. The sun made rainbows in the spray. He looked up as I walked over. I didn't want to appear too eager. I wasn't sure if we'd still get on and thought we might have to start fresh all over again.

"Early morning shower," Skip shouted, waving the watering-can. "Might help the spinners later. Too easy otherwise for the batsmen."

I nodded. There was no need to worry. We just carried on from where we'd left off. He told me to bring over a heavy plank of wood. He placed it carefully on the wicket and told me to jump up and down on it.

"Heavy roller," he explained. "That's the light one over there." He pointed to a thin plank. The score-boards were blank and behind the bowler's arm lay a score book and two freshly sharpened pencils and an eraser. At the top of the page Skipper had printed:

FIRST TEST. SYDNEY, AUSTRALIA. 1932.

AUSTRALIA v ENGLAND.

Skipper seemed to believe everything about the game was real. I couldn't have done that in case I looked a fool. But Skipper seemed completely unafraid of being laughed at. I don't think he even thought about it. When I'd finished "rolling" the wicket I tried to lift the piece of wood at one end but it was too heavy.

Skipper came twinkling over, dragging his legs behind him.

"Here," he said and lifted the plank as though it was a pencil. I suddenly realised how strong his wrists and arms must be. People whose legs don't work are often like that.

Mrs Skipton came out with a pair of scissors. She cut some flowers and put them in a bucket. Her hair was drawn back tight into a bun and it shone in the sun. She smelled nice and her hands were long and pale. There seemed to be something sad about her. Maybe it was because of Skipper being ill or maybe because of her husband. Whenever there was a break in the game she'd bring out two glasses of orange juice and some biscuits.

"Tea interval," she'd say. Never made fun like some mothers would. She was always very serious about anything Skip did.

Every morning, for three weeks of that hot summer, I would run through the trees to that lawn and there would

37

be Skipper in a white sun hat and a short-sleeved cricket shirt painting in the lines on the crease or watering the wicket. He seemed to know everything about those days.

"Do you know that Larwood used to wear a metal plate on the toe of his boot because he banged it down so hard?" he'd say. Or out of the blue as part of his commentary he'd let you know that Grimmett, the Australian spin bowler, used to practice with a tennis ball on a carpet at home when he was a boy and that he could make the ball land on one spot and bounce up and down there till it stopped. He had hundreds of books about the Bodyline series. Soon I knew almost as much as he did about those cricketers of long ago. We'd spend hours on those days when it was too cold to play, sitting in his front room arguing about who should be in the best World Eleven. Then we'd write them out in our best handwriting and alongside their names we'd write their autographs. When we'd finished, we'd read out the names like they do on the wireless: Bradman, Jardine, McCabe, Kippax, Hammond, Paynter, Oldfield, Voce, Larwood, Bowes and so forth. It was almost like praying. And so the games we played on that sunlit lawn became real for me too. At first I'd pretended to believe it but inside I knew it was only a miniature game. I could see from the start that it meant everything to Skipper. He took it all so seriously, I suppose, because of his legs and because he couldn't play real cricket. But, by the last day of that First Test, if someone had told me we weren't playing on a sun baked wicket in Sydney with the crowd on the Hill shouting and barracking, I would have been really surprised. That's how real it all became to me. Soon I was commentating as hard as Skipper. I seemed to be spending my whole life there. I didn't have to tell my mum where I was going every morning, she'd know. Sometimes as I ran out of our gate I'd shout out, "Just going to Skipper's," and she'd give a kind of nod. Once I was on that lawn the rest of my life seemed to be far away. I suppose you could call it magical. I sometimes thought it was *too* good or else a kind of dream; that one morning I'd arrive and there wouldn't be any trees or lawn, no Skipper waving as I emerged out of the wood. But it was real all right. After three weeks with Skipper in that sheltered garden that we called Australia, I even found it difficult to talk to anybody else. I met John Eccles one afternoon on my way home and he'd been my best pal at school. I just couldn't think of anything to say and we stood around making boring remarks. He'd never even heard of Larwood. Outside that garden was like being abroad. We'd even developed our own way of talking, Skip and me, so that anything else seemed strange. We'd talk in a kind of shorthand. Nobody else would have understood it. But we knew. Without trying we somehow seemed to know what the other was thinking. All the time Skipper would suddenly say something that I was just thinking in my head. It was almost frightening. And we enjoyed speaking where we finished each other's sentences. He'd start and it would go like this:

"Dry
Today
Very
Roller
Light I think
Spin later
Of course

Naturally
But Victory
Will soon be in sight
Said the blindman."

That's how we'd talk half the time.

I only missed one day in that three weeks and that was to go for the County trial. I would have almost rather played our game with Skip but he persuaded me to go. He said it was important. England needed a good number four, he'd say, though Compton was showing promise. He had ambitions for me but I knew I wasn't that good. He kept going on at me to practise. He was more pleased than me, I think, when I did reasonably well and got picked twelfth man against Shropshire Boys. Skipper made his mother promise to let him go and watch if he was feeling well enough. He even made me bring over the letter. It was creased and dirty with me reading it so many times:

"We are pleased to inform you that you have been picked to play 12th man for the County Schoolboys against Shropshire Schoolboys on the 3rd of August . . ."

He even kept the letter and pinned it on his wall. I think he was more excited than I was.

I think Mrs Skipton liked me to come round.

"Skipper looks much better," she said. She'd make me sit down and talk to her. She spoke to me as though I was a sort of friend, a grown-up.

"He never had many friends because of missing school. Haven't you any friends? Are you neglecting them?"

"I like coming here," I told her.

She used to tell me her life story. She had lived in America for the first twenty-two years of her life. She'd met Skipper's dad when her father had come over to work for the Embassy in London. He was something to do with the Navy. She didn't mention her husband at all. I really liked to hear her talk. Most grown-ups spend most of the time telling you what not to do but she kept encouraging me to go out and do things.

"Go west, young man," she'd say. It became a catch phrase between us. She seemed really interested in everything I was doing and never made me feel I was being a nuisance. She made me feel that everything I did was important.

"Gee, that's interesting," she'd say.

Or, "Golly gosh, ain't you the smart cookie." Soon we were all saying "golly gosh".

When she laughed, too, she'd throw her head right back and really roar. Nobody had ever laughed like that at anything I'd said. I was glad to make her laugh because sometimes when she thought you weren't watching she had a way of looking terribly unhappy. I really wanted to help her.

One day we went to the beach in Mrs Skipton's Humber. She was a really good driver. Inside, the leather seats smelled hot and she sang us a song about some poor little lambs who had "gone astray". She didn't sing in a proper way. Like, I used to hate the way our music teacher Miss Fountain used to sing at school. She always clasped her hands in front as though she had the belly ache with her mouth moving about all over the place showing her gums and her eyes closed half the time. I hate that kind of stuff. Mrs Skipton sang sort of straight out and really loud. You couldn't say it was a beautiful voice but it was strong all right. Really strong. At the end she'd laugh. You know, really hearty. Skip would sing along in a way that was out of tune but went together. I hate singing normally. Can't seem to get my mouth open properly. I'm always coughing and looking round to see if anybody is watching. Maybe I'm embarrassed because my dad sings on the train sometimes. Really loud hymns and things. It's dead embarrassing, especially if there are kids from school in the carriage. I look out of the window to try and show we aren't related and I just happen by chance to have sat next to him. If he speaks to me and gives the game away I just laugh as if he's a stranger. When we arrive at our stop I realise they'll all know I'm with him so I get up first and say, "This is your stop." As if he's a poor old man I'm helping. Sometimes I wish I was an orphan.

> "Poor little lambs
> Who have lost their way
> Baa baa baa."

I loved singing that song. When we went past our house I could see my mum coming out of the kitchen door with a bucket. She didn't see me.

The wind washed the smell of summer and green grass in through the open windows and it mixed with the smell of leather. Skipper would give his cross-eyed look at school girls on bicycles and talk about them as if they were "toenails".

> "Baa baa baa"

I sang at the top of my voice.

Mrs Skipton would laugh along and then, just as suddenly, this sad look would come over her face, really sad. As though she'd never smile again. Skip didn't seem to notice too much. Maybe he was used to it. Or perhaps he pretended not to notice so as to keep it from me. I'd tell really stupid stories to Skip, all sorts of daft things but really they were aimed at her. I couldn't stand to see her unhappy. When I get to be eighteen, I thought, I'll marry her. Then, I thought, I'd end up being Skipper's dad. I started laughing to myself. When Skip asked me what I was laughing at I couldn't tell him. I suppose it was because it was to do with his dad. He was funny sometimes about that. So instead I sang,

> "We're dear little toenails
> Who have lost our way."

And Skip laughed anyway.

"Here's the beach," said Mrs Skipton and straight away this sad look left her face and she started laughing again. We whistled over the sand. It seemed to stretch for miles. Skipper had Sophie on his lap. As the car swung about he started doing his daft commentary, like the cricket commentary only more stupid.

"And the car's swinging about and Sophie's falling out. No, not quite. She's been rescued." He held her up in the air. Sophie laughed and gurgled. She got so excited on one corner that she piddled all over Skipper's pants. He wasn't worried at all. He just carried on.

"And yes, Sophie's laughing, ladies and gentlemen, and she's done a piddle. She's done a great big piddle over Skipper's pants."

Things like that he was doing all the time. Mrs Skipton didn't seem to mind like some grown-ups might. She never said things like, "That'll do" or, "Just behave".

She stopped the car. There were only about three people about. A horse-drawn ice-cream van went past and disappeared behind one of the dunes. We sat there in

silence for a bit just looking at the sea. The car smelled of salt and seaweed and leather. Mrs Skipton turned round in her seat.

"Want to give it a go?" she asked.

"What, drive?" I said. "Honest?"

"Sure, why not."

I climbed into the driving seat and she sat beside me and told me what to do. The beach was deserted now so there was no danger. After a bit I started to get the hang of it. It was a great feeling. Three weeks before I'd never even been in a car and now here I was driving one. Skipper couldn't drive it because of his legs. Maybe it was a good job. It would be just like him to drive it into the sea and try to reach America or something. I drove back to the shelter of the dunes and Mrs Skipton chose a good spot for a picnic. She spread out a cloth and we had sandwiches and two sorts of cake. She'd also made some flapjacks. They were American and really sticky. I'd never tasted them before. Then Skipper started digging a hole while his mother had a sleep. I thought he was never going to stop. Then he stopped and did this mad face as if he was listening.

"Hear that?" he said.

I listened.

"Australia," he said. "We've come out right under the Melbourne wicket."

"Imagine our two heads popping out," I said.

"Toenails," he said and we both rolled about laughing.

Mrs Skipton woke up and asked us if we'd like an ice cream. The van wasn't in sight any more so she let me take the car. As soon as we were out of sight of her, Skipper asked me to let him drive. Of course he couldn't work the pedals properly because of his legs. I had to lean

46

across while he did the steering. At first he was very serious. Concentrated. Then suddenly, without any warning, he spun the wheel round and we went round and round in circles leaving deep trenches in the sand. It was like being on a merry-go-round. I shouted to him to stop. I was beginning to feel sick. He didn't take any notice.

"Golly gosh, gee," he shouted.

Even though I was feeling queasy I couldn't help calling out, "Ain't I the smart cookie."

He didn't seem to have any fear at all.

"Faster," he'd shout, "faster." But I was scared he might crash the car. I couldn't press the pedals properly to get up a good speed so he made me crouch on the floor and press them with my hands. It was quite frightening going along and not being able to see where we were going. Course the next thing is, Skip starts doing this mad commentary pretending he's Malcolm Campbell breaking the land speed record.

"And he's up to a hundred miles an hour."

I eased my hand off the accelerator.

"More speed, more, more," he shouted. My hand was aching like mad.

"Skipper Campbell, the fastest driver in the world even though he has no legs." He was always making jokes about himself like that.

"And it's Bluebird," he screamed, "up to one hundred and twenty miles an hour."

We were actually doing about thirty, if that. It felt a lot faster because I could hardly see where we were going. I wasn't too worried though because I knew I could always ease my hand off the accelerator and we'd slow down. Then I felt something pressing down on my wrist. It was

47

Skipper's foot. He was just letting it bear down on my wrist. He pressed harder and harder. He'd slumped down in his seat. From the outside it must have looked really funny. This car tearing across the sand with just the top of a ten-year-old head peering through the steering wheel.

"Get off, get off," I shouted, "you'll crash us man, don't be mad."

At the same time, even though I was scared, I was having hysterics. Really uncontrollable laughter, like you do when you're scared and laughing all at the same time. And Skipper was rattling on at his crazy commentary. He'd just seen the horse-drawn ice-cream van.

"And it's No Legs versus the ice-cream van, neck and neck," he shouted. He swung the wheel over really hard. His foot pressed down on my wrist. I couldn't move it. It hurt really bad. But there was nothing that could stop Skip now.

"Give over Skip, you loon, we'll be killed."

I managed to pull my head up enough to get a glimpse of what was going on. It was true, the ice-cream van, pulled by this tired-looking pony, was ambling along. The driver had a droopy black moustache and was wearing a flat white hat. He was singing very loudly in Italian. He was very happy. He had no idea what was about to happen, otherwise he wouldn't have been singing. I ducked my head down. I couldn't bear to watch. If I was going to be killed I'd rather not see.

Skipper said, "And there could be a head-on smash between Bluebird and the Italian ice-cream van." Skipper slumped even further down in the seat. His face was almost next to mine. He looked at me and suddenly closed his eyes.

"And the driver of Bluebird has suddenly been struck blind."

He really didn't know what he was doing.

I poked my head up as far as I could. My eyes were just able to see over the dashboard.

"Skipper, give over." I tried to wrench my wrist away but there was no moving Skipper.

"Do you turn the wheel right to go right?" he asked very calmly.

We were hurtling straight at the ice-cream van.

"Right," I shouted, "turn the wheel right."

"And the driver has gone deaf as well as blind," shouted Skipper.

Then the horse saw us. The sight of this driverless car rolling straight at him in the middle of a calm summer's afternoon was just too much for the old nag. He thought his time had come. His eyes rolled in terror and up went his front legs. The Italian stopped singing quite suddenly and looked very serious. The horse came down on to his front hooves again sending sand splashing up. He pulled back his lip, bared his yellow teeth and then he set off down the beach like something on the last furlong of the Ice Cream Grand National. The owner was hanging on for dear life and there was a lot of ice cream on the beach. Then we suddenly stopped. My head hit the dashboard. The reason we'd stopped was we were trying to dig our way into a sandhill. The car stalled. I got out to have a look. Just before the end we had been going quite slowly so there didn't seem to be any damage. I wondered how many miles away the ice-cream van was by now. I picked an ice-cream cornet off the sand, blew away the sand, and me and Skipper ate it. Skip could hardly speak for laughing. He kept thinking of the horse's face and he burst into laughter again. I brushed the sand off the radiator and mudguards, reversed the car out and drove back slowly to where Mrs Skipton was waiting for us. I thought we must have been away for hours but it could only have been about ten minutes.

Skipper's mother stood up and brushed the sand off her white dress.

"I was going to buy you an ice cream but the van galloped by in such a hurry," she said.

I started giggling behind my hand and pretended to look at something interesting in the sea.

"Wonder what made him do that?" said Skip innocently.

We clambered into the car and drove back home through the country lanes. On the way we stopped and picked some bilberries. Our finger tips turned purple with the juice. Skip's mother said she'd make them into jam. The sun sank low behind the trees. The tar on the road had melted with the heat and you could smell it. We all sang at the top of our voices:

> "We're poor little lambs
> Who have lost our way."

The tyres crackled on the cinder path of their front drive. "Baa baa baa," we sang.

There were a lot of days like that.

Chapter Four

That afternoon England were in deep trouble. The main problem was the injury to Larwood. According to the rules, which seemed to get more complicated every time we played, a player was injured if the "ball" knocked him over twice during the same innings. Of course he'd be back for the next Test but in the meantime England were already two to one down and if they lost the Melbourne Test the series would go to Australia. Voce was fast all right, but he wasn't as fast as Larwood. How could you replace the fastest and most terrifying bowler who had ever walked on to a cricket pitch? When Bradman heard that Larwood was out of the Test he must have slept easily in his bed for the first time in months. The great Australian run machine could walk to the wicket knowing he would not see that fearsome figure curving in towards him, the head up, the short brown hair brushed back. He could take guard with confidence knowing that the ball would not be whistling round his ears with the speed of a shell. We put Larwood beneath the trees where we could watch the match. Yes, losing Larwood was a bitter blow for Jardine and the England team. I patted the crease. I was Bradman. I'd started batting yesterday and played through until bad light had stopped play. I was seeing the ball well during the first few overs of the morning and with a bit of luck might well take my not-out overnight score of one hundred and fifty over the two hundred mark. Neither of us had ever reached two hundred before.

To give the England spinners more of a chance we brought on the watering-can for a light shower. No roller of course. Bradman settled down. Skipper tossed the marble from hand to hand and moved Jardine in a couple of inches. The light was perfect.

"Jardine's face a study in concentration now. He must be worried at the way Bradman is seeing the ball but that recent shower may have given the spinners a chance."

With a flick of the wrist Skipper released the ball. It bit into the newly-watered pitch, gripped, turned and rose viciously off a good length, rapping Bradman on the pad.

"HOWZATT!" shouted Skipper. I wrung my hand painfully.

"Out!" said a voice. I hadn't spoken; neither had Skipper. I looked in the direction of the house but Mrs Skipton had gone shopping, taking Sophie and the dog with her. A loud laugh came from the direction of the trees.

"Didn't you hear me? Out," it said.

We both looked towards the wood. There in the shadow of the birch stood, of all people, Sawbridge. My heart dropped. Sawbridge was a big kid with glasses who used to go to our school. He was about two years older than me and at one time I used to go round with him. Well, not really go round with him. Nobody who didn't have porridge between his ears instead of brains would have Sawbridge as a pal. But if you had the bad luck to be chosen as his friend you didn't have much choice. You could say no but then he'd beat you up. Being his friend wasn't much better because he was always thumping you anyway or saying stupid things. Not that Sawbridge ever actually spoke to you, I mean not a conversation. He used to speak in these quick sort of bursts and then laugh all down his nose. Talking to Sawbridge was like having a conversation with a backfiring motor bike whose nose was blocked up. And whenever he got to the end of his remarks he'd just thump you and give this snort.

"Taters, gis yer apple. Schnoff, schnoff, schnoff. Bash yer if you don't, schnoff, schnoff, bash bash."

After five minutes with Sawbridge you were one big bruise and inches deep in snot. He wasn't what you'd call Prince Charming.

How I came to go around with him for a couple of weeks was that he picked me for his team one afternoon break. Every break at school we had this game of football with a tennis ball. It used to run all term. By the time the holidays came round the score would be something like two hundred and thirty goals to two hundred and forty seven. You weren't supposed to change the teams but because he was bigger than anybody else Sawbridge would start the game all over again if his side were losing and he wanted some better players. We played right across the playground and the goals were two dustbins at either end. Everybody took it dead serious though and there were often fights about the score. My pal, John Eccles, played goalkeeper and kept score because he was good at adding up and was the only kid in school with gloves. Sawbridge had about as much idea of playing football as last year's tapioca pudding but if you didn't do what he wanted, he'd twist your arms up behind your back until you thought they were going to crack.

"Does it hurt, Taters, schnoff, schnoff; does it hurt?"

So you tended to do what you were told. This afternoon he got fed up with losing, he and John Eccles picked

54

sides. We always picked sides by having the two captains walk towards each other heel and toe; the last one to get a whole foot on the ground got first pick. I was hoping like mad that Eccles would get first pick because I knew he'd have me in his team. But my luck was out. His toe just trod on Sawbridge's. When they saw Sawbridge had first pick everybody put their hands in their pockets and started looking at the sky or the floor because no one wanted to be in his team. Anyway the first name he called out was mine.

"I'll have Taters, schnoff, schnoff, schnoff." So that was it.

Sawbridge always played centre forward.

"Me centre forward," he'd shout. All through the game he'd be bawling out for the ball.

"Here, here, over here. Gis the ball. Gis the ball," so you could hear him in the next county. And when he got it he'd just set off like a steamroller with glasses, knocking everybody out of the way until he hit something that he couldn't knock over. Like the lavatory wall, though he had a fair go at that. It was really boring. If he scored he'd run around all over the place waving his arms in the air, shouting, "Goal, goal," and thumping anybody he could reach half senseless. My feelings about Sawbridge were that he'd be better off with a ring through his nose standing in a cage at the zoo so that he could make the gorillas look handsome.

Anyway on this particular day I had the bad luck to play well. The ball came to me deep in our half near the staffroom and I beat a couple of men, bouncing the ball off the wall and collecting the rebound. I raced off towards their goal. Out of the corner of my eye I could see

Sawbridge charging down the middle like a demented ostrich with specs, screaming.

"Taters, Taters centre, centre. The head, man, the head."

In his wake was a line of wounded, groaning opponents rubbing their heads and arms and legs. It was like a battlefield. I looked up and thought, "Right Sawbum," (that's what you called him when you wanted to annoy him or were out of distance). "Right Sawbum, you want the ball, you're going to get it." I drew back my foot and let it fly as hard as I could. I couldn't have met it cleaner. The tennis ball flew through the air like a shell. There was a terrific crack as the ball hit him just above the ear before cannoning past Eccles's gloved hands and into the toilet wall for a goal. The force of the cross had pole-axed Sawbum. He lay on the floor for a few seconds, not moving. That's it, I thought. He'll murder me for that. At first I thought I'd killed him but then slowly he pulled himself on to his feet, put on his specs and lumbered towards me. The idea of running came into my head but my feet didn't seem to be interested. I could feel my arms aching already. I was hypnotised by his face. It floated towards me getting bigger and bigger. Then his nose was touching mine. I could see his eyes all swollen up behind his specs. Then his eyes sort of disappeared and a great crack appeared in his face. I couldn't believe it. Sawbum was smiling. Sawbum was pleased. He thumped me so hard on the back I thought my chest was going to shoot out of my nostrils.

"Magic pass, Taters," he screamed, covering me in spit. "Weouoough, smash, GOOOOOAAAAAL." Sawbum was very pleased.

He walked back to the centre spot holding my arm up

in the air shouting, "What a winger, schnoff, schnoff, Stanley Matthews. Weough, smash goal."

The worst thing imaginable had taken place. Sawbum liked me. He wanted me for his pal. It was frightening. For the next couple of weeks he was my best friend. Or at least he thought he was. If you wanted to grow up with two complete arms it didn't pay to cross Sawbum. He went everywhere with me. Waited for me after class. Walked home from school with me. Stood next to me in assembly. He even invited himself to my birthday party which he wasn't supposed to know about but he happened to see a couple of other kids pulling my hair in the playground. He just kept fighting with everybody and used our new sofa as a trampoline. After they'd had the springs repaired my mum and dad made me promise never to see him again. They said he was a bad influence. I didn't need them to tell me that. But getting rid of Sawbridge wasn't as easy as all that. Luckily it was nearly the end of term when all this happened and by the next term Sawbridge would be in the big school so we sort of drifted apart. But I still wore the bruises that proved Sawbridge had once been my best friend.

Now there he was, skulking in the bushes, just when Bradman had a chance of scoring a double century. It was like being on a picnic, just about to tuck into the jelly and trifle, when suddenly you look up and there's a mad bull pawing the ground where the meat paste sandwiches had been. I couldn't believe my bad luck.

Over the last couple of years, Sawbridge's arms had got longer and he'd grown about six inches. He'd also grown about two hundred spots on his face. He certainly hadn't got prettier. He gave us a big grin, and started pulling a comb through this black hair that looked as though a three ton truck had just emptied a load of Brylcreem on to it earlier that morning. He pulled out a packet of Craven "A" cigarettes, stuck one in his mouth and lit it. Like I said, Sawbridge was no Prince Charming.

"Taterchips," he barked, "you was out." Calling me Taterchips was his idea of wit. Before this conversation was over he'd have gone through every variety of potato that had ever been invented. He came lumbering towards me out of the shadows.

"Here, you was out, man."

"No I wasn't," I said.

"Course you was."

He crouched down and stuck out his finger as if he was an umpire giving me out.

"Tatermash," he snorted, "I'm giving you out. And when I gives you out, Tatermash, you have got to go."

I looked over towards Skipper but he was looking at the ground, not saying anything. I'd learned from experience that the best way of keeping out of trouble with Sawbum was to humour him. If I could get him in a good mood he might leave quietly.

"How did you get in?" I asked him lightly. I knew I mustn't let him know that I was frightened.

"Followed yer in, didn't I," he said. He looked round, taking in Skipper and the emptiness of the house. He took a cigarette packet out and offered me one. "Ciggy," he said. I didn't dare refuse. He struck a match and lit me. I took a deep drag to show him I was used to smoking. Then I started coughing. Sawbum slapped me on the back.

"Never smoked before?"

"Course I have," I lied, trying to take a drag without it going into my lungs. Sawbum smiled at me, cupped his hand round his cigarette, inhaled deeply and blew streams of white smoke out of both nostrils. He went to the pictures a lot, did Sawbridge. He spat through his teeth on to the wicket.

"Followed you in, din I. Sees you going over the wall. Thinks, hello, where's Tatermash going?"

He looked over at Skipper who was still looking at the ground. He wouldn't do anything while there were two of us. Once he saw Skipper's legs, though, anything could happen. I prayed that Skipper would have the good sense to keep them hidden. Once Sawbum saw that he only had me and a cripple to deal with, he'd start thumping us. That was the kind of hero Sawbridge was.

Skipper brushed his long hair out of his eyes. It was the first movement he'd made. Even though he was stupid, there was a kind of sharpness about Sawbridge. When you most didn't want him to see anything he'd notice. Now he looked hard at Skipper.

"Who's yer girlfriend?" asked Sawbridge, pointing with his cigarette at Skipper and laughing his snotty laugh. For Sawbridge that was probably his best joke of the year. I knew I had to stick by Skipper no matter what happened. I knew that was more important than anything. I looked Sawbum straight in the eyes.

"He's my friend," I said. Still Skipper wouldn't look up. He seemed to be shaking slightly. Shivering. I didn't want to believe that he was frightened. Sawbridge noticed it too.

"Your friend eh," he said, "what's he shaking for then. Not afraid of me is he? Not afraid of old Sawbridge, is he?"

Skipper didn't move. Didn't say a word.

"Course he's not," I said.

Sawbum put his arm round my shoulders. I could smell the grease on his hair and the tobacco on his breath. I threw my ciggy away. It smouldered in the grass.

"Well, this is my friend," said Sawbum, squeezing me so hard that I gasped for breath. "Used to be in my team at school, didn't you, Taterpie?"

I tried a wan smile. It wasn't enough.

"My pal, aintcha? Down the wing. Bang. Goal!"

"Yes, I'm your friend, Sawbridge," I said, as calmly as I could. While I was saying this I was trying to think of some way of getting him out of the garden. But it was difficult to think while a Brylcreemed gorilla was doing his best to squeeze the life out of me. He smiled and let me go; then looked round and picked up Jardine in his fist.

"What's this stupid game? This ain't no game. This is really stupid, schnoff, schnoff."

I explained patiently. "It's miniature cricket."

Trying to be sensible with Sawbridge was like trying to teach a rhinoceros to tap dance.

"Cricket," he snorted, "cricket. Here, I wanna game."

I looked at Skip. After all it was his game. His garden. But I could see he was too afraid to talk. His eyes stared fixedly at the ground. Sawbum dropped Jardine on to the ground. He snatched the bat off me and held it with his great fist as though it was a frying pan he was considering doing a murder with.

"Got to have me go, int I," he said. "Titchy bat innit?"

If only Mrs Skipton and the dog would come back. That would get rid of him. But there was no sign of them. I decided to argue gently.

"We're in the middle of a game, Sawbum." The name

60

slipped out. He clutched me by the throat. "What did you call me, Taterpie?"

"Sawbridge," I told him, "I called you Sawbridge." His eyes stared into mine. His face close.

"Yeah? Well you'd better." He let go of me.

"We'd really like you to play, Sawbridge, but we're in the middle of this game. Skipper's mum and the dog will be back any minute." I tried to make it sound more like a piece of information than a threat.

"Dog eh?" He looked round and thought about that for a moment. There was no sign of anybody. He glanced over towards Skip.

"This is Skipper then, is it? Don't say much, does he?" Skipper stared blankly at the ground. Because Skipper didn't say anything, I just began to talk.

"This is Skipper. His dad was the captain of a ship. He got torpedoed. He was killed." As soon as I'd said it I kicked myself. I suppose I said it in order to impress Sawbum. Of course it just made him worse.

"Oh yeah," said Sawbum, and for the first time he looked straight at Skipper. But Skipper still kept his eyes on the ground. I could see his hand trembling. As long as he kept his legs still. I prayed silently.

"Your dad a hero then is he, Skipper? Din do him much good in the end did it? Schnoff schnoff."

I was disappointed somehow that Skipper was so afraid, though I could understand it. What could he do with his legs against somebody of Sawbum's size?

"Look here, hero, aintcha gonna let me play?"

He was looking for a reaction, pushing it, pushing it. He didn't know where but he kept on pushing just to see what would happen. Skipper remained silent. Sawbum gained in confidence.

61

"What's up with the hero?" Nothing from Skipper. If only Mrs Skipton and the dog would come back.

"Can't your friend here speak or something?" He was getting more and more aggressive. He crouched down in front of Skipper and stuck his neck out so their faces were only inches apart.

"Funny looking nerk, aintcha? Why dontcha get a haircut?"

Silence.

"Here, what is it? A boy or a girl?"

Skipper didn't move. Sawbum lifted Skipper's head by the hair.

"Excuse me miss," he said, "give us a kiss," and he laughed.

I could feel myself beginning to get angry but I didn't really want to start anything. Then I heard a voice, loud and clear.

"Leave him alone, Sawbum." I looked round and realised it had been me. Sawbridge turned on me.

"What did you call me?"

"I said, leave him alone, Sawbum."

His face went red. He was dead angry. I was for it. I put my arms up to protect my face. The next thing I knew I was on the ground. There was a numb pain in my jaw and my face seemed to be covered in water. I brushed away the water wondering where it could have come from. My hand was red. The pain made my eyes water but I wasn't crying.

"What you call me?" repeated Sawbum. He was on top of me turning me on to my front. My nose was in the dirt and he had both arms up somewhere near my neck. I thought they were going to crack any minute.

"What you call me?" he kept saying over and over and

63

each time he said it he jerked my arm. I cried out in pain. Then suddenly I was rolling free. I couldn't understand it. Perhaps I was unconscious. My arms had no feeling in them. I looked up. Sawbridge was lying on the ground about three yards from where Skipper had thrown him. He turned round and picked up his glasses.

"Here you . . ." he began. But he was more wary. Skipper tried to struggle to his feet. For the first time Sawbridge could see his legs. A big smile broke over Sawbridge's face when he realised he was dealing with a cripple. He clenched both fists. He was going to enjoy this. But Skipper's voice stopped him in his tracks. He spoke very slowly and clearly as though Sawbridge was a simple child.

"I wonder if you'd be so kind as not to roll your big ugly body all over our cricket pitch."

The way he said it almost made me laugh. I was used to the way he talked but to hear him talking that way to Sawbum just sounded so funny. Sawbum didn't think it was funny though. For a minute he just stared in amazement. Then he gathered himself together.

"Who d'you think you're talking to?"

Skipper looked round as though there might be somebody else in the garden. Of course, apart from us three, there was nobody.

"I can't see anybody else, can you, so I suppose it must be you." Sawbridge looked like a mad dog who's just about to bite somebody when they suddenly produce an ice cream and say, "Ice cream for the nice doggie." He couldn't understand what was going on. Slowly his brain turned over, clunk clunk, and it dawned on him that he was being made fun of.

"I'd be careful who you was talking to if I was you,"

he snarled. "Specially with your legs. What d'you think you can do to me, cripple?" He spat out the last word.

Skipper's face didn't change. Very calmly he said, "Do to you? Well, I'm not very interested in you really but the game has reached a very intriguing stage and your lying about all over the pitch does rather prevent us from continuing, so I'd be obliged if you'd get up and go somewhere else." He paused and raised his eyebrows. "Like Alaska, for example." Skipper gave a really sweet smile.

Clunk, clunk. Sawbum's brain started turning over again like a run-down steam engine.

"What if I don't go, cripple. What you gonna do about it? You gonna make me go? Are you? What you gonna make me go with, eh? Gonna kick me, are you? Is that what you gonna do? Kick me with them legs?"

The feeling was starting to creep back into my arms. I was working out how I was going to throw myself on Sawbum if he went for Skipper.

"No, I won't kick you," said Skip, even and cool. I knew he was trying to think of something, trying to trick Sawbum.

"No, you better not neither," said Sawbum. "Ain't got no choice anyway 'cos I'm going to thump you anyway."

Skipper was still cool. He spoke as though he was telling his mother he'd rather have jam than marmalade. "Well, if you insist on fighting, I suppose there's nothing else for it."

"You and whose army?" said Sawbum.

"The question is," said Skipper, "what are we going to fight with? You don't want to fight with legs, though I would have thought kicking was more your line."

"I don't need to kick you, cripple. I could beat you easy . . ."

"With one arm tied behind your back," said Skipper, before he could finish.

I cottoned on to what Skipper was doing. Sawbum fell right into the trap.

"Yeah," he said, "with one arm tied behind my back."

A gleam came into Skipper's eye, half amusement, half a kind of triumph. It was the sort of look he wore when he was opening the bowling with Larwood and you knew that in a couple of seconds the ball would be singing around Bradman's ears at about a hundred miles an hour. It was a look I had learned to become wary of. He came in very quickly.

"One arm behind our backs. That suits me fine."

For a second Sawbum hesitated. He too smelled something going on but his brain was too slow to work out what it was. But it was only for a second.

"Arm behind the back?" he repeated.

"Yes, one arm wrestling. Unless, of course, you're afraid."

"Afraid?" snorted Sawbum. "Me? Afraid of a cripple?"

Skipper, still smiling faintly, shifted on to his side. He put his left arm behind his back and raised the other, resting on his elbow with the palm open and inviting. Sawbridge came over slowly and took up the same position. They turned their heads towards one another. For what seemed an eternity they stared into each other's eyes. Then slowly their hands clasped tight. Sawbridge was smiling. Skipper was playing for time. It was clever of him to do that but after Sawbridge had won I knew it wouldn't end there. He'd turn on me.

"Skipper," I said, "let him have a game."

Skipper didn't move or say a word. His whole attention was on Sawbridge. He smiled, then said to me, "If you'd be so kind as to be umpire." His eyes never moved from Sawbridge's face. "Elbows mustn't leave the ground. Watch for that, umpire." I crouched down.

"Best of three?" I asked.

Skipper laughed that laugh of his.

"Oh no," he said, "Only one. We'll only need one, won't we?"

"Yeah, one'll be enough to finish you off," said Sawbridge and he smiled.

There was a silence. They looked at me.

"Ready?" I asked. They both shuffled a bit. Sawbum licked his lips. My hands were hot. I could feel the sweat on my forehead.

"One, two, three. GO!"

Sawbridge's face strained and he pushed with all his might. He grunted with the effort. Skipper's face wore no expression at all. He could have been a statue cut out of stone. All the effort was inside him. But his eyes never left Sawbridge's. It was as though Sawbridge was a book and Skipper was trying to read it; searching for a sign of weakness. And yet he looked almost mild. In a strange way, amiable. Sawbridge grunted once more with the effort. His teeth were bared. His wrist and hand trembled as he pushed with all his might. Slowly, terribly slowly, Skipper's hand started to go down.

Sawbridge snarled through clenched teeth. "When this is over, cripple, I'll thump you and all." He meant it too. I wanted to encourage Skipper. Inside I was willing a strength into him but because I was umpire, I didn't dare say anything. Skipper would never have forgiven me. To do that would have made us no better than Sawbridge.

67

Skipper made no sound. The veins stood out on Sawbridge's forehead. Snot was coming from his nose. The two wrists were trembling. If Sawbridge really does go for Skipper, I thought, I'll pick up the plank we use as the heavy roller and lay him out with it. Skipper's wrist crept further and further down. It was almost on the grass. Through the grunts Sawbum was beginning to smile. His face was pink with the effort. He hadn't expected such a struggle but now he could see he was going to win. Skipper's knuckles were almost touching the grass.

"Come on, hero, you haven't got your dad to help you now," hissed Sawbridge.

Skipper's expression didn't change.

My own wrist was aching just with thinking about it. I clenched my fist as if I was fighting too. It began to tremble with the effort. Then something strange happened. My arm went completely weak. It was as if all the strength had drained out of it. I wondered where it could have gone. I felt faint. I took a deep breath and wiped the sweat off my brow. I looked at Skipper. His mouth had stopped smiling. It was straight and humourless. For the first time he was really trying. Slowly his hand pushed upwards. Sawbridge couldn't resist it. Soon the two hands were upright. Suddenly I realised where my strength had gone. Why I felt faint. It had gone out of me and into Skipper. Sawbridge didn't know this but he was fighting both of us. I didn't really understand it. I wouldn't ever be able to tell anybody what was happening. Nobody would believe it. I didn't understand it but somehow I knew it was true. For what seemed an age the two hands trembled upright and unmoving. Sawbridge's eyes were closed with the effort. Then his hand, very slowly but in one continuous movement, began to go down. Just before his knuckles touched the ground, his eyes opened. There was a kind of panic in them. Then, it was over. His wrist was flat on the grass. He tried to get up but Skipper held him pinned there. He had something to say. I clenched and unclenched my wrist. Slowly the blood and strength returned to it. Its job was done.

"No," said Skipper, "I'm not a hero but my father is. I don't like to hear his name in your mouth. It dirties it. Do you understand?"

Reluctantly Sawbridge nodded.

"Do you understand?" He pressed down. Sawbridge winced.

"Yes," he mumbled, "I understand."

Skipper held him for a few more seconds. His eyes never left his face. Then he let him go. Sawbridge rolled away, rubbing his wrist. He clambered to his feet. Once there, he knew Skipper wouldn't have a chance. I thought to myself, he shouldn't have let him go. I threw myself forward but Sawbridge flung me aside. He stood over Skipper with his feet astride then lashed out with his foot. I turned away. I didn't want to see it. There was the sound of flesh on flesh. I looked. Skipper had caught him by the ankle. Slowly, using both hands, he began to turn it. Harder and harder, further and further. Sawbridge cried out in pain and anger. Then he tumbled to the ground. He was on his back with Skipper on top of him. Skipper held both of his wrists hard and slowly began to bring them together above his head. Sawbridge cried out.

"Don't, it hurts!"

Skipper was still calm.

"I think," he said slowly and softly, "it would be a good idea if you were to leave here now because, when you've gone, the air will smell a great deal more pleasant."

"Geroff, geroff," panted Sawbridge.

"So, if I let you go, will you promise to leave and never come back?"

"Geroff."

"If you don't, I shall be forced to break both your wrists and I'd really rather not do that."

"Geroff."

"Promise."

There was a pause. Sawbridge turned his head left and right.

"All right," he said.

"Good," said Skipper and rolled off.

Sawbridge scrambled slowly and painfully to his feet. For a minute I thought he was going to go for Skipper again but then he thought better of it. There was something in Skipper's eyes that made him change his mind. He turned and stumbled towards the trees. He bent down. I wondered what he was up to. When he came up again I could see he had the injured Larwood in his hand. He made a movement as if to break it.

"I should put that down, if I were you," said Skipper, and something in the tone of his voice made me shiver. Sawbridge stared for a minute and then, reluctantly, dropped the figure. He turned to go, then offered one last shot.

"You wait, Taters," he shouted at me. "I'll get you. One day I'll get you."

Then he was gone, stumbling through the trees.

Skipper was already replacing the scattered fielders.

"And Bradman's ready to take guard once more," he said in his commentary voice. It was as though nothing had happened.

"The drunken Australian supporter has been removed from the ground."

I picked up the bat. Settled down and took guard.

"And it's Voce coming in to bowl to three men on the leg side crouching close."

I squinted down the wicket. The ball zoomed through the air and took my off bail. Skipper raised both hands in jubilation.

"And Bradman has gone. Bradman clean bowled by Voce. The speed of that ball took the bail thirty feet."

The dog Hamish romped round the side of the house followed by his wag and Mrs Skipton with a basket.

"Everything all right?" she called.

Skipper raised his head. "Bradman's just gone to Voce," he said.

What a friend, I thought to myself. What a friend.

Mrs Skipton put the baby down.

"Ain't he the smart cookie," she said.

We looked at one another and said at exactly the same time.

"Golly gosh, he sure is."

Then Skipper laughed that laugh of his.

Chapter Five

Lightning seemed to crack open the sky and the rain beat down so hard it bounced inches off the pavement. I hurried down the road, my gaberdine mackintosh over my head. It was the day after the game with Shropshire. My luck had been in. Being twelfth man I hadn't expected to play but a boy called Farnworth, who went to a public school, had broken a leg in a climbing accident in the Cairngorms, so I got my chance. I batted number eight which was rather low since I'm supposed to be a batsman but it worked out well for me. Because I hadn't expected to play and nobody was really expecting me to do anything, I felt relaxed. Skipper's mother took us both and Hamish and Sophie came too. I kept telling Skipper it was a waste of time them all coming because I'd only be twelfth man but he was sure I'd get a game.

"It's in the stars," he said. "D'you think I'd come all this way if you weren't going to play?" I couldn't think of an answer to that.

One side went in first and there was a bit of a collapse. By the time it was my turn to bat we were forty for seven. As I walked out, Skipper said, "Straight bat and keep your eye on the ball."

I looked round and took guard. I had three more balls to play in that over. A big lanky kid I'd heard them call Grant was bowling. He smiled at me in a superior kind of way and threw the ball from hand to hand with a kind of twist. He did it without looking. I'd have to practise that when I got home. He'd just bowled out two of our players consecutively. There was only me between him and a hat trick. My dad said we couldn't afford cricket boots so I was wearing plimsolls. I heard this Grant say, "I'll drop one on his feet, that'll make him jump." I looked round the field. I felt really important with everybody watching me. But half of me was wishing I was at home. I could see Skipper in his chair near the pavilion. Could see him gesturing and saying something. I knew what it was, even though I couldn't hear. I straightened my bat slightly and waited. The lanky kid took a long curling run towards the wicket. His face was red with the effort. The ball came through like a red blur. I'd never faced anything so fast. I knew I mustn't back away. I'd rather get hit than back away. I put my left leg down the wicket in the direction of the ball and leant my bat into it holding the handle loosely so as to kill the ball. It turned in and struck me on the pad. The lanky kid leapt into the air. "Howzatt!" he screamed. He'd been rehearsing that appeal at home. I looked at the umpire. He was looking in the sky as if he was watching a parachute coming down and shifted a pebble from one pocket to the other. Two balls to go.

"This chap's a bit of a rabbit," said the kid, Grant. It was meant to be loud enough for me to hear. One of their slip fielders said, "Rabbit, rabbit." They were deliberately trying to put me off. The wicket keeper started laughing.

I settled down again. I wondered what Skip was thinking. I felt I was batting for the two of us. In came the bowler. He was going to put everything into this one. As

he released the ball I heard him grunt with the effort. I swung my bat but just missed connecting. The ball thumped into the wicket keeper's gloves. The bowler appealed again. This time for a catch. We both knew I hadn't touched the ball. "Jammy bugger," he said when the umpire gave me not out. I didn't seem to be able to hit the ball. What if I was out, I thought. Out for a duck. No I couldn't, not in front of Skip after he'd come all that way. Then suddenly something happened. I started thinking how Skip might have played this bowler. And I didn't know how to explain it but it was as if Skip was inside me. Not just speaking and giving me advice but as if half of him was me. I could hear his voice doing this commentary. The way he did when we played on his lawn.

"And it's Tattershall taking guard. He looks supremely confident. The bowler comes in and Tattershall leans forward into that one. A beautiful off drive and it flashes to the boundary for four runs."

There was a sound of the sea breaking. I sort of shrugged myself awake. The ball was bouncing off the rails and the crowd was applauding. It was as though I'd done it in my sleep. The bowler stood panting with both hands on his hips. He couldn't believe it. I thought of saying something like, "Not bad for a rabbit." But I knew Skip wouldn't have liked it so I just smiled at this bowler and he stalked off into the covers, tugging on his cap. After that everything seemed to go my way. The ball looked as big as a football. I didn't seem to be able to miss. In the next over I scored eight and went on to make forty-seven not out. Thinking I was Skip gave me a kind of confidence I'd never felt before; it gave me style. The match ended in a draw but I knew I'd done well enough to be picked for the next match. Skipper looked as pleased as though he'd scored the runs himself. I wanted to tell him that in a way he had. But I kept quiet. We rode home in Mrs Skipton's Humber through the early evening, singing and going over the game.

Now it was the next day and the weather had changed. Even though there was no chance of us finishing the Test I was going over to Skip's anyway so that we could talk over yesterday's game. Skip would remember every ball. I ran through the wood. It was so thick there that the rain could hardly come through. I kept running because I knew you could get struck by lightning in a wood. I could never remember if you were safer under a single tree or in the middle of a wood. I ran as fast as I could to be on the safe side. The thunder cracked and roared as though it was a few inches over my head. At the edge of the wood I paused to gather myself for the sprint across open ground to the house. The pitch was a lake. I lifted up my raincoat over my head. It was dark as night. Then in a flash of lightning I saw the man. I was partly dazzled but when the light gave way to darkness again he was gone. I was sure I'd seen him. He wore a trilby and a pale raincoat with the collar turned up. He was deathly pale and there was a terrible sadness in his eyes. And something else, something about his skin. Something strange that I couldn't describe. Almost as though you could see through it. As I stood there, dumbfounded, I wondered whether he had been there. Perhaps I'd imagined it all. Certainly there was nobody there now. I looked around. The thunder rolled and rain dripped like a curtain off the leaves of the trees. I shrugged my shoulders and sprinted round the lawn leaping over the biggest puddles. I could

feel the damp coming through my shoes. When I got home, my mum would tell me off for not taking my wellingtons.

Skipper was in the front room. The Monopoly board was laid out and there was a fire burning in the grate.

"Weather," I said.

"No play today."

"Australia under water."

"Toenails," we both said together.

For a time we talked about the game against Shropshire. I took my shoes and socks off and dried them on the hearth. Then we started to play Monopoly. I didn't say anything about the man in the woods. It just seemed silly. Skipper played Monopoly like he played everything else. As if his life depended on it. His eyes hardly ever left the board. Occasionally they flickered up to me. Soon he had hotels all over Mayfair and Piccadilly as well as Leicester Square and The Strand. All I had was The Old Kent Road bit and Waterworks. In the end he even made me sell him those. He was without mercy. A few times I tried to give in when I saw I had no chance of winning but he wouldn't let me. He didn't crow though. He just didn't know any other way to play. After he'd bankrupt me completely he didn't exactly say he was sorry but somehow showed that he knew that perhaps he'd played too hard.

"You'll be able to play plenty of times," he said, counting up his money.

It was a sort of explanation. At that moment I didn't really understand it. The rain stopped and Mrs Skipton brought in milk and biscuits on a tray.

Skipper looked out of the window. Although there was only a light drizzle it was far too wet to play and the sky was still dark. Mrs Skipton had switched the lights on. I could see Skipper's reflection in the window. It merged in with the lights, the rain and the trees outside. He looked almost like a ghost. I munched my biscuit, looked into the fire and wondered about the man I'd seen. I looked back at Skipper's ghostly reflection in the glass. Thunder rumbled far off towards the seaside. There was something I wanted to say. Something about his face but I didn't seem able to work it out. It was like something I could only half remember. Like a name that you can't quite bring back. It was funny. Skipper turned round slowly. He caught me looking at him. I felt I shouldn't have been. I felt it was something you shouldn't do. There was a half smile on his face.

"I played well yesterday," he said quietly.

I wondered if he was thinking the same thing I was thinking. He went on.

"When you were out there batting, I sort of thought myself over to you. It was as though I left my body and these rotten old legs behind." He laughed.

I couldn't think of anything to say. Skip must have seen my amazement. He laughed again.

"You too?"

"Yes," I said.

"Tell you something," he said, "I felt it was me scoring all those runs."

There was a silence.

"What does it mean?" I asked. We were so close it almost frightened me. It was like a dream.

"Shall I tell you something else," he said. He turned again to the window and traced his finger slowly down the glass; studied what he'd drawn.

"When that ball hit you on the pad."

"Yes," I said.

He turned and faced me. "I felt it on my leg."

"Felt it?"

"Yes," he said.

For what must have been a full minute neither of us spoke. The wind rushed through the leaves making a sound like a river and somewhere in the garden the dog barked.

"What does it mean?" I asked again. Skipper shrugged. I told him how I'd felt when he was fighting Sawbridge. How the strength had seemed to go out of me. I couldn't look in his face while I was telling him but poked the fire gently. The fire spurted into fresh life.

"Maybe we're one person," said Skipper.

I laughed. It wasn't a real laugh but one of those that's supposed to show you're not nervous. Skipper saw through it right off though.

"Are you scared?" he asked.

I stopped laughing. He just kept laughing at me so I laughed again.

"Are you?"

"No," he said, "I've never been frightened." He didn't say it in a show-off way. Just very simply so you knew that it was true. He shuffled over to where I was sitting. The fire crackled in the grate. It threw a red glow on his face.

"Shall I tell you something I often think?" he asked.

I nodded. I was too bewildered to say anything. I felt like you do at school when you're being told off, and your face goes all hot, and you can't seem to speak properly. Skipper seemed much more at home in this experience than I was. He perched his elbow on his knee

81

and stared into the fire as though there was something written there that he was reading.

"I often wonder if people, other people, see the same things as me."

I frowned.

"You know," he went on, "how do you know that the red you see is the same red that I see or that anybody else sees?"

I couldn't believe it. I'd often thought the same thing. I felt a bit daft about thinking it so I'd never bothered to tell anybody else in case they laughed.

I said, "Maybe everyone sees something different. Maybe there are as many reds as there are people."

"That's what I thought once," said Skipper. "But since yesterday, I know. I know that what you see is what I see. What you feel."

"Yes," I said. I took a deep breath. "I sometimes wonder if all the people around me are like me. I mean real. Or perhaps . . ."

"They're just outsides."

"Yes," I said. I started to feel really funny. Like I had when I saw my mum crying in church when we went to bury Grandma. Skipper put his hand into his pocket and pulled out a clasp knife. It was black and the blade was very curved. It had his dad's initials on it. He opened the blade. I thought he was going to ask me to cut my arm so that we could be blood brothers, like in the film I'd seen at the Plaza last year when the Cavalier had saved his enemy's life and they really liked each other even though they were on different sides. I didn't want to do that. It was the kind of thing that really stupid kids did. I didn't want Skipper to be like that. Skipper looked at me and smiled, then he closed the knife slowly. It clicked back into place. It was a great knife. There was a long silence. Skipper broke it. He clambered on to the sofa and stood up.

"This is my ship," he said holding both arms out. He pointed to the carpet. "That's the Atlantic." He put his hand round his mouth and swayed from side to side as if the sea was rough. "All right, Mr Mate, bring her to starboard." I was used to Skipper's sudden changes of direction. He was always coming up with a new idea and I was content to follow. There in that dark living-room, with the thunder still rumbling and the rain beginning to come down steadily again, we played out the last voyage of Skipper's father. But it wasn't a game. Not a real game. The more it went on the more real it became. The sofa stopped being a pretend ship. It *was* the ship. The carpet became the grey and heaving sea. And when the torpedo struck, Skipper tumbled gasping from the sofa. He struggled and fought for breath as though he was really drowning. Suddenly I realised he wasn't acting. His face had gone a deathly white and there was a purple colour about his lips.

"Skipper! Skipper!" I shouted, but he just groaned and his head rolled from side to side. I stood there for a moment staring then ran out of the room.

"Mrs Skipton! Mrs Skipton!" I ran through the house screaming. She came out of her bedroom and looked over the bannister. She was wearing a full-length, pink housecoat.

"It's Skipper," I shouted. "He doesn't seem to be moving."

She raced down the stairs. Skipper was lying on the carpet as I'd left him. She knelt down and pulled his head up so that he was leaning heavily against her with his

83

head thrown right back. His mouth was open and spit was coming out of it. Mrs Skipton spoke to me very calmly but I could tell she was frightened.

"Go to his room," she said. "By his bed you'll see some green pills and a glass of water. Bring them."

I dashed upstairs. I knew which pills they were. It was funny being in Skipper's bedroom without him being there. The room didn't know he was ill. I dashed back with the pills. She snatched them from me. His mouth was clenched and his eyes were closed. I couldn't see him breathing. She forced her fingers between his teeth, pulling them open, unscrewed the bottle and put one of the pills on his tongue. Skip's eyes opened for a moment.

"Swallow it," she said. "For God's sake, swallow it!" She placed the glass of water against his teeth and tipped it. Skipper choked and gasped. Some of the water went down. Mrs Skipton was almost rough with him. She put another pill down his throat. "Come on," she kept saying, "come on!"

The blue colour started to go out of his lips and his breathing became easier. His eyes were closed but I knew he wasn't asleep. Now and then he opened them to look round but he didn't seem to know where he was. Mrs Skipton cradled him as if he was a baby, stroking his hair. She lifted him on to the sofa. I stayed with him while she went to fetch a blanket. By the time she came back, he was sleeping. She laid the blanket over him and watched him for a bit then she beckoned for me to go out with her. We went as quietly as we could. She took me into the kitchen and told me to sit down. Mrs Skipton looked at me for a moment. Some of her hair was coming down on to her forehead. Usually it was swept back and there wasn't a hair out of place. She went across to the

refrigerator and poured me a glass of milk. I held it cupped in both hands. It was really cold. Mrs Skipton tucked her housecoat in tight beneath her neck and folded her arms.

"He's going to be all right," she said. "He'll sleep now."

She lit a cigarette and blew the smoke away from me.

"I want to know what happened," she said. I'd never heard her so firm.

"It's important, you see, that I know."

"Yes," I said. I didn't know what to say. I wanted to be helpful but I didn't want to get Skip into trouble. I didn't know how I was going to tell her about his dad.

"What happened in there that made him so excited?"

"We were just playing," I said.

She drew heavily on the cigarette.

"Just playing. I see. What were you playing?"

"Games," I said, "Monopoly and things."

"Just Monopoly?"

"Sort of," I mumbled.

"Sort of." She started to look angry. "*This* isn't a game, you know. What happened to Skipper is very serious. I'm sure you want to help him, don't you?"

I nodded.

"The best way you can help is by telling me everything that happened."

I looked down at the floor and played with the glass. Rolling my finger round it.

"We played a kind of acting game," I said.

She snatched the glass away from me. "What sort of acting game?"

"A sort of war game. It was only daft."

"Tell me."

It felt stupid telling her about the game. It didn't feel the same in words as when we were playing. I wondered whether I should tell her about what we'd talked about but then I thought I was in enough trouble already. She tapped her cigarette out briskly on the ashtray.

"Well?" she said.

"Well, it was a sort of war game at sea. Skipper was the captain and we were hit by the torpedo and the ship went down." I shrugged. "It was only a game."

There was a silence. Then Mrs Skipton said, "You're leaving something out." It was like being in court. I couldn't answer. "Tell me," she said.

"Well," I said, "we were on the ship and when it went down Skipper pretended he was drowning. Then he couldn't get up. I thought he was acting but then I could see he meant it so I came for you."

She looked at me without blinking. She was going to drag it out of me.

"Is that all?" she asked.

I lifted my eyebrows. "Yes," I said. Then to be on the safe side I added, "I think so."

"Are you sure?" I felt that she knew there was more and that she knew what it was and that I knew she knew.

"I want you to tell me everything. You want to help Skipper don't you?"

There was no escape.

"Skipper was pretending that he was his dad." It came out in a rush. "I suppose he was acting out how he got killed."

Mrs Skipton sat still for quite a long time. I could sort of hear the silence drumming in my ears. Then she got up and looked out of the kitchen window. The rain was still falling. I wasn't sure if she was crying or not. I hoped she wasn't. I couldn't stand the silence.

"It was only a game. He fell on the carpet. Then he was very pale. Really pale. He looked like the man."

Mrs Skipton's head came round.

"What man?" she asked.

"In the wood."

"You saw a man? In the wood? When?"

"Just before."

"Before when? What are you talking about?"

"Before I came in today." She leaned on the table. Her eyes looked strange.

"You saw a man here this afternoon and didn't tell me."

"Perhaps I didn't."

"What d'you mean?"

"It was dark. There was lightning. I saw this man. But I'm always imagining things and thinking they're real. Like when I thought I saw some Vikings on the beach and my mum said . . ." I wasn't sure now whether I'd seen him or not.

Mrs Skipton grasped me by the shoulders hard.

"Did you see him or didn't you?" I remembered the flash of lightning and the face. I nodded.

"What did he look like?"

"White, he was very white. He hadn't shaved. And the side of his face. It was all funny."

"How funny?"

"Like shiny. As if you could see through it."

Mrs Skipton held me harder. Then she suddenly turned and ran out into the rain. I followed her. I saw her run across the lawn. There were white splashes in the dark where she went through the puddles. And then she was

88

gone. There was just the sound of the rain and the wind roaring. I was cold. For the first time I started to think how good it would be to be home. I strained my eyes in the darkness but I couldn't see her. The rain ran down my neck. I thought of my mum and dad sitting at the tea table. There was a sudden cry. Three rooks crashed up out of the trees, cawing loudly. I shivered and turned towards the porch. A hand dropped on to my shoulder, making me cry out. I looked round. It was Mrs Skipton. Her hair was soaked and plastered down on to her head. Her housecoat was clinging to her. She didn't seem to mind how wet she got. Her eyes stared straight ahead. Hearing about the man must have really frightened her. She walked past me into the house. I followed her. She was sitting at the table, not moving. My teeth were chattering but she didn't hear. I coughed. Started to explain.

"I don't think there was anybody. I imagine, you know, things. Like these Vikings." My voice tailed off.

She didn't seem to have heard. Just sat there looking at nothing. I could hear the rain dropping off her hair on to the table. Then she looked up at me and gave a funny sort of laugh. I suddenly saw her like she must have been when she was a little girl.

"Yes," she said, but I knew she hadn't heard really.

I wanted to go over and tell her it was all right. She ought to have called the police. I thought, my dad would know what to do. I wished he had been there. Thinking of that, and our warm kitchen, I said, "I'd better be going home."

She showed me to the door. For the first time I went round the path. All the way home I kept seeing this strange face.

I didn't tell Mum or Dad about what had happened. Mum told me off for about ten minutes for being late for tea and for getting wet. She made me change all my clothes while Dad rubbed my hair dry. When he'd finished my head was spinning. I had welsh rarebit on toast with H.P. sauce all over. In a way I was glad I got told off. I don't know why but I was really glad.

Chapter Six

I didn't go over and see Skipper the next day or the day after that, and anyway it was raining. On the afternoon of that second day, my mum and dad took me to town shopping. I usually hate going shopping with them because they make you wear all these stupid clothes that you'd never buy if you were on your own and then there's a row and they keep apologising to the shop assistants for your behaviour, and all the way home on the train nobody speaks and my mum keeps adjusting my dad's overcoat collar or spitting on a handkerchief and rubbing your face. How would they like it if I went out and bought them clothes they didn't like? But on this particular afternoon they were in a good mood, and after what had happened at Skip's I was quite pleased to be out with them and kept talking to my dad so he didn't have a chance to sing on the train and embarrass me or anything. Anyway my dad bought me a proper pair of cricket boots with toe caps and a row of shiny studs underneath. My dad had never been any good at sport himself and he'd never really been interested in my playing, though he'd always ask how I'd got on. But I could see that he'd been impressed by these letters from the County Selection Committee that were typed out on thick white paper with an address and a crest at the top. I think for the first time he was proud of me, though he could never tell me straight out. Buying the boots was his way of showing it. He even told this shop assistant.

"They're for the lad. He's playing for the County you see." He said it very casually as though he didn't care but I could see he did. It made me blush, but I didn't mind too much. I wore those boots in the garden when we got home that afternoon and cleaned them about three times with white stuff even though they weren't really dirty. I even wore them in bed that night. They were great boots.

After tea I decided to go over and show them to Skipper and anyway I wanted to see if he was better. The sun had come out but the ground was still wet. Too wet to play anyway. I stood at the edge of the wood for a minute and thought about the man I'd seen. I thought I heard something behind me. I couldn't make my head look round but when I did there was no one there. It was different in the daylight.

Skip's chair and table were in their place but I couldn't see any sign of him. I wondered where he was. Hamish came romping over, wagging his tail and nearly twisting himself back to front. He licked my hand and barked and then ran off in the way that dogs have; as if there's an important meeting to go to. I walked over to Skipper's chair. On the table with his medicine was a metal tin with the lid open. I peeped inside. There were six small sticks. When I looked closer I realised it was the spare set of stumps for the miniature cricket. By the side of the tin was a bottle of paraffin and a box of matches. While I was trying to work all this out, I heard Skip's voice shouting my name. He was close by but I couldn't see him. I looked all round but there was nobody in sight. A small twig fell on my shoulder. I looked up and saw the soles of a pair of shoes. Above the shoes, looking down, was Skipper's laughing face.

"Always said I'd get to the top!" he shouted.

"What about your legs?" I said. I couldn't believe he'd climbed the tree. I'd have had a job even with arms and legs.

"Legs," he said. "Oh, I took them with me." He let go both legs and swung there whooping. He was just like Cheetah in that Tarzan film my dad had taken me to see the year before at the Bedford in Birkdale.

"You'll kill yourself," I shouted. He laughed at that. I wondered how he'd get down off that last branch. It was about eight foot off the ground and he wouldn't be able to land properly with his legs.

"Catch me," he said.

I stretched my hands up. His legs felt really thin, like broom handles and they swung all loose as if they were on hinges.

"Ready?" he shouted. I wasn't a bit ready. I'd never caught anybody jumping out of a tree before. He was hanging full stretch from his arms. He said, "The password is toenails."

I said, "Toenails" and, just as he was about to let go, these terrible giggles started. Once I start giggling I can't stop. Then Skipper caught them off me. There was me on the ground giggling like mad, staggering about and going red with trying to stop, and Skipper hanging like a monkey laughing his head off.

"Wait," I said. But it was too late.

"Ready?" he said.

"No," I said. But he couldn't hang on for laughing. He landed right on top of me, knocking me to the ground. For about five minutes we just lay there, rolling about and laughing so much we could hardly get our breath. It was one of those laughing sessions where it really hurts and you want like anything to stop but you can't. Whenever we nearly stopped and were just getting our breath back and gasping one of us would say, "Toenails" and we'd be off again screaming and rolling about and holding on to our stomachs. When we finally stopped I was aching all over. Skipper was staggering about but still laughing. Eventually he collapsed into his chair.

"Did you really go to the top?" I asked.

"Course I did. Great view. I could see all the pitch. Just like a grandstand."

He picked up the metal tin and started breaking the wickets. He poured the paraffin over the broken pieces. I asked him what he was doing. He looked at me mysteriously.

"It's The Ashes," he said.

I didn't know what he was on about.

"Ashes?" I asked.

"Not ashes," he replied. "Not any old ashes. *The Ashes*."

I still couldn't understand him.

"The Ashes that England and Australia play for."

"Ah," I said.

"Come on," he said and walked to the edge of the wood. "Here's a good place," he said, and started digging a hole with his clasp knife. "You dig now," he said. He was getting tired, I could see. While I was digging he took a match from the box and dropped it into the tin. The paraffin flared up blue and violet then settled down to a rosy flame. He came over and placed the tin with its lid closed in the grave I had dug. He was breathing as though he'd just run a race.

"You cover it up," he said and went to sit in his chair. When the grave was filled in he threw me a wooden cross and told me to stick it on top. On the cross he'd burnt out with a hot poker the words:

IN MEMORY OF AUSTRALIAN CRICKET
WHICH PASSED AWAY ONE AFTERNOON
IN SYDNEY, AUSTRALIA. FEBRUARY 1933.

R.I.P.

"What's R.I.P.?" I asked Skipper. There was no answer. When I looked round he'd fallen asleep. I wondered if he was all right. I thought, he shouldn't have climbed that tree. I started to walk across to the house for Mrs Skipton when I saw her walking across the lawn.

"Time you were in bed," she called across to him.

She looked at Skipper, put her hand on his forehead.

"What happened?" she asked.

"He fell asleep," I said.

"Had he been doing anything to tire himself?"

I couldn't tell her about the tree. She'd have gone mad. I couldn't think of anything to say.

"We were laughing," I said.

She looked at me. She was surprised but she wasn't angry. She smiled.

"Laughing makes you sleep does it?" She was frowning but she was only pretending. Skipper turned over in his sleep. I could see he wasn't ill like he had been the last time. Just tired.

"We'd better take him in the house," said Mrs Skipton. "We'll make a chair."

We lifted Skip out of his chair and carried him carefully

into the house. We put him down on the sofa and he opened his eyes and winked at me. I winked back.

"Drink this," Mrs Skipton said. Skipper took the glass and gulped down the medicine. Then he lay back and closed his eyes. It started to rain again. The room was getting dark.

"I'll make a fire up. He can sleep here tonight," said Mrs Skipton. She asked me to go to her room and bring an eiderdown and two blankets that were in an ottoman by the wall, while she looked after him.

I went up the stairs. It felt strange going into her room. Everything was pink and the carpet was so thick you could feel yourself bouncing up and down on it. I lifted the lid of the ottoman and took out the blanket and the eiderdown. The room smelled of powder and scent. There was a pair of white, high-heeled shoes under the bed and a painting of a boy in a blue suit, blowing bubbles. I was just turning to go when something caught my eye that made my hair stand on end. On the bedside table was a photograph. A photograph of a man. Somebody ran a cold finger down my back. I looked round with a scream. There was nobody there. Goose pimples had come so suddenly it had felt like a hand. I picked up the frame. I was shaking. There was no doubt about it. Although he was wearing a peaked cap and was clean-shaven, I was certain it was the same man I had seen that time in the wood. I looked at it for a long time. Then something else hit me. That feeling I'd had as I was looking at Skip's face reflected in the window. That sense that there was something I couldn't quite put together. Now I knew what it was. The face I had seen at the edge of the wood and Skip's face. They were almost the same. Skip's father.

But how could I have seen him when Skipper had told me he was dead?

"My husband," said Mrs Skipton. She took the photograph from me.

"It's the same man," I said.

"The same man?" she frowned.

"That I saw in the wood."

She had gripped my wrist so hard it was aching. I caught sight of my face in the mirror. It was as white as a sheet. She said, "I must look after Skip, keep him warm."

We walked down the stairs together. When we were half-way down she sat and pulled me down beside her.

"I think I ought to tell you all about it. Just wait here."

She went into the living-room where Skip was. He must have woken up. I could hear their voices. I heard her tucking in the blankets and sheets round him. I sat quietly. There was a grandfather clock in the hall. It tocked loudly and you could hear the pendulum swinging backwards and forwards. The voices had stopped in the living-room. Mrs Skipton came out. I half stood up but she sat down beside me. We both looked straight ahead. Then she looked at me.

She said, "Look, I'm very sorry all this has happened. I know it can be frightening."

I just kept looking at her.

"Look, I'm going to tell you something and I want you to promise me never to tell anyone. Not even your mother or father. Do you think you can do that?"

I nodded and swallowed. I was frightened but at the same time I felt important too.

"Not even Skip. Promise."

My fingers almost slid up to give the cross my heart sign but I knew this was too serious for that.

"Promise," I said.

"The War started when Skipper was about three years old and it's true his father was in the Navy. We'd always done a lot of sailing and men like that were needed when the War began. He wasn't a captain though. He was second officer. One night in the channel his ship *was* torpedoed. But it didn't go down. Five men were killed but my husband wasn't one of them thank God. He came home on leave. Although his face had been badly burned it was the effect on his mind that was the most serious. You see, he'd been very shocked by what he'd seen. He used to say that the men who were killed were somehow lucky. How terrible the injuries had been. He had very bad nightmares. Nearly every night he would wake up screaming."

I thought of Skipper's father, with his face transparent with burns, in the room I was in, screaming. I thought of the one pair of shoes I'd seen under the bed. Mrs Skipton lit a cigarette. She cleared her throat.

"After his leave was over and he'd recovered from his injuries, he had to go back to sea. At least I thought he'd gone back. Then one afternoon an officer came round from the naval department. Skipper's father hadn't returned to his ship. He had run off and was in hiding. He couldn't face going back to war again. They'd come to see me because they thought that's where he'd be. He daren't come back, even now, because they'd put him in prison, you see, and I think that might kill him."

When she first began to talk her eyes had been on me but now they seemed far away. There were still things I couldn't understand.

"Why did Skipper tell me he was dead?"

She brought her eyes back to me.

"Oh you can understand that, can't you? Skipper worshipped his father. Every boy wants his father to be a hero, doesn't he?"

I thought of my dad that afternoon telling the shop assistant about me and my cricket. I wasn't sure what it meant to be a hero. I thought of the stories I sometimes told about my dad being injured in the War.

"Yes, I suppose so," I said.

"You see Skipper would much rather have his father dead than a coward. Somebody who left us both. If his father is dead he can remember him as he was."

I was trying to work out how Skipper, who told the truth about everything, who you couldn't tell a lie to because he'd see right through you, could be guilty of telling me such a big lie. I thought that I ought to turn away from him but somehow this weakness made me want to be with him more. It somehow made him more like me. Made everything else about him bigger and finer.

Mrs Skipton stubbed out her cigarette. "Now you do understand, don't you, that you mustn't say anything to anybody about what I've said tonight. Especially don't let Skipper know I've told you. It would be very bad for all of us. If he found out that I'd told you, it might become very difficult. Your friendship means a lot to Skipper, and to me as well of course. You may think it's strange because I'm his mother but I think we both realise that Skipper is somebody exceptional. I'm sure he'd become . . . he'd do something in the world, if only . . ." She broke off. "You see, because of what has happened, we're rather . . . cut off. So you've been important to us." She put her hand on mine and smiled. I could see Skip's face in hers. That same smile. Sort of far away. Suddenly she was brisk and business-like.

"I have to make a phone call now. I'm going to leave you to think about what I said. If you want to know more, ask me. I'm afraid I've put a burden on you telling you all this. Having a secret like this is a terrible thing. It can weigh you down. I'm sorry I had to do it but there was no other way. I'll always tell you the truth, you know."

I smiled but it was one of those smiles that switches itself off very quickly. This wasn't something to smile about. I had a lot to sort out. I wished I could have done something for her, to help her, but I didn't know what. She went down the stairs and into the dining-room between the living-room and the kitchen. I heard the phone being picked up. Everything was turning round and round in my head. The dog came up the stairs, stopped, licked my hand and then went down again. I decided to go home. I didn't want to see Mrs Skipton again. I wanted to leave everything as it was. It would be wrong somehow to say goodbye or anything, so I decided to creep down the hall and out into the back garden through the kitchen. I hoped she would understand that I wasn't just creeping off but that I was doing it for a reason. I came down the stairs. Skipper was in the doorway of the living-room holding himself up. His face was white and set. He looked at me for a long time without moving. Then his face broke. It was like one of those masks. He pushed it right into mine.

"You never saw him," he hissed. "You never saw my dad. He'd never do a thing like that. It's a lie. It's a lie. It's a lie. He's dead. I know he's dead. How dare you think he did that. He's dead, dead, dead. Get out of here. Get out. I never want to see you again!"

"Skipper," I said, "don't. I won't tell anybody. I promise I'll never tell anybody. I'd rather die than tell anybody!" But he wasn't listening.

"Get out, get out and don't ever come back."

Mrs Skipton came through the door. She must have heard the screaming.

"Get out," Skipper screamed.

I pushed past them both, turned, and walked through the kitchen into the garden. I was mad. Really mad. If he didn't want to see me again, well, that suited me fine. Catch me going back there again. What had I done? Anybody would think I'd murdered somebody. Murdered somebody by bringing them back to life. I stormed into the garden. It was then I noticed something about the pitch. Even though I was angry I went to look closer. Where the wicket had been was a large hole and some of the players had been snapped in half. I heard a rustle in the trees and saw a shadowy figure slipping away. Cigarette tobacco. It was Sawbridge. Although it was dark I was sure that it was him. I didn't run after him or try to catch him. The moon floated out from behind a bank of cloud. The garden turned white. I had a feeling that something was ending.

Chapter Seven

For the next two weeks I concentrated on keeping my place in the County side. I went to nets practically every evening and worked really hard at my batting. Some nights the First Team players from our village team would come over and bowl at us and I could feel myself getting better, especially against fast bowling which had always been my weakness. We played a couple of games, beat Shropshire in a replay, and won our way through to the semi-finals. Our game was to be played at our local village ground. I would have liked Skipper to be there but I couldn't bring myself to go round and see him. It was him who had told me not to come back, so I reckoned it was up to him to patch up our quarrel. Mainly though, it was pride that stopped me from going round. As the time passed, the reason for our break-up didn't matter as much as the fact that it was difficult to make it up. It was like at the baths when you don't want to dive in because the water's going to be dead cold. You know that once you've got in it'll be all right. Once Skipper and me started talking everything would be fine, it was just getting the courage to plunge in that was difficult. Without Skipper I knew there was something missing; a kind of emptiness that wasn't just to do with him but with the garden, the game, his mother, the car rides, the seaside trips and the orange juice. All of those things. When I looked back on the times we'd had it was almost like a taste. Like remembering the flavour of a banana or bacon and egg. Another thing: England had managed to win that Fourth Test, even without Larwood, and we'd only played one day of the Fifth when the rain started. I was sure Skipper would hate leaving the series unfinished, maybe even more than I did. I had no one to talk to any more. I sometimes went to John Eccles's house or played over the sandhills; but it just wasn't the same. With Skip I only had to say a word or even give a kind of look and we'd both know right off what the other was thinking. I thought, I'll never get that with anybody else.

Anyway, when I knew where our semi-final was going to be played, I wrote him a note. I put it in one of my dad's brown envelopes and walked over to their house. I crept up the drive, dropped it through the letterbox and ran back down the gravel path, through their gate, and hid, looking through the hedge. It was the first time I'd ever been up to his front door. The Humber was parked in the front drive and Hamish the dog was mooching about, sniffing drainpipes and looking miserable. I felt really strange being a kind of outsider watching all these familiar things but somehow not able to go in. I couldn't help wondering what Skip would be doing. It would be dead easy to knock on his door. But then I thought, what if he doesn't answer it? Or, worse still, opens it and then just shuts it in my face without saying anything. And even if he didn't slam the door, what could I say to him? I couldn't say I was sorry because I hadn't done anything wrong. And I couldn't stand there and say "Skipper, let's be pals again." I'd have felt a right custard. So I just hid behind the hedge and waited. The door opened. It was Mrs Skipton. The brown envelope was in her hand. She looked up and down the drive. I felt rotten somehow, crouching there when I could easily have got up and gone over to her. She closed the door and I went home.

Whether he read the note or whether they spoke about it, I don't know, but he never came to the game. I'd been averaging about twenty-eight which wasn't bad so they'd moved me up to my best position in the order which was four. I knew I had to play well enough to play in the final. I thought that if we could get there, Skipper would really enjoy it. We'd play Yorkshire on the town ground. It had a proper pavilion and you had to walk down steps and through a little gate when you went in to bat. Another thing, there was a chain fence all round the boundary. Skipper would have had me practising opening the gate properly and rehearsing how I carried my bat and looked round at the fielders. It would be great walking out to bat at eleven o'clock in the morning just like in a County or Test match. At that time the grass would be still wet. I started getting butterflies in my stomach just thinking about it. If we did get through Skipper would be going round telling me the names of all the great players who had ever played for Yorkshire. Yorkshire was his favourite team. He used to say, "Nobody else really plays cricket except Yorkshire."

Well, we managed to win that semi-final. It wasn't a great or exciting game and in a way we didn't deserve to win. I made fifteen, which I thought would be good enough to keep my place, especially as most of the others got less. But we would probably have lost if Geoff Poole, our best batsman, hadn't made forty-three not out. Anyway the main thing was that we were in the final. After the game I was given my white cap with a crest and the name of the County on it. Tommy Dutton who played for the village First Team came over after and told us we'd won only because Sussex had dropped all their catches. Then he said, "It's a sign of a good team when they can play badly and win." I suppose that was right. We were all excited about playing the great Yorkshire team in the final. They'd won the cup for the last three times and we'd never even got to the semi-finals before. One or two of their boys had gone on to play in the County team. Just to play against them, whether we won or not, would be exciting. Of course we were all hoping we could win.

It was about half-past six when I left the ground. Instead of going out of the front entrance and down the main road, I took a short cut across the ploughed fields of Batty's Farm that came out on the canal. It half crossed my mind to call in at Skipper's and tell him about the final but I was still mad at him for not coming to the game when it was so close. I thought, well, it's up to him now. I'd written him a letter. In a way I felt stupid, writing him this letter and then have him ignore it. I thought if I went to his house, he'd probably do the same thing and shut the door in my face. I wouldn't give him a chance.

Where the field ended there was a slope down to the canal. I scrambled down it. My head was full of the final. In the olden days they had horses going along the path pulling barges. Mr Haggitt had explained it to us the day we went on a history trip and it rained. After a bit the path came to a long tunnel. The path was made of flagstones and you could hear your footsteps echoing as you walked along. The tunnel was so long you couldn't see the light at the end and there was water dripping off the damp walls. It was a pretty frightening place normally and I'd never have gone down there but I didn't want to be too late home. I wanted to keep my dad in a good mood by getting home as early as possible. I didn't want there to be any trouble about the final. If he was in a good mood I'd be able to ask him if I could stay out later than usual. So, even though I was a bit scared, I carried on. Something fluttered past my face. It was a bat. I hated bats. I kept my right arm over my head in case one flew into my face. About ten years before there had been a murder in the tunnel. It had even been in the *News Chronicle*. One of the lock keepers and his wife had been found by a schoolgirl. There was a story going round at school that some nights the dead lock keeper could be seen steering a barge through the canal. One of the kids at school said his mum had seen it once and had fainted. They said the man's wife had been floating in the canal face down with her arms stretched out. When they turned her over the rats had been at her face. I tried not to think about it. There was a scuttling sound and a plop. A rat dived into the water. I walked a bit quicker. The path curved slightly and I was relieved to see a pinpoint of light in the distance.

It was then that I heard it. I stopped and listened. Footsteps. There was a roaring in my ears. I walked on and stopped again. Maybe it was the echo of my own footsteps. I stopped once more. The other footsteps stopped. It was my imagination. Then there was the sound of something heavy falling into the water. It made waves. I thought of the lock keeper's wife. In my mind's eye I could see her in the dirty water floating face down. She turned over and there was no face. I began to whistle. Then I listened. The same whistle came back at me out of the darkness. It sounded awful. The whistle stopped. There was a silence and then it started again. It seemed to be behind me. I looked back straining to see but it was too dark. The whistle stopped. Silence. Just the water dripping off the roof. I started to walk and the whistling began again. I could feel my skin wrinkling with goose pimples. The whistling stopped. There was a silence then something rattled past my feet and into the canal. I began to walk away from the whistling as quickly as I could, towards the light at the end of the tunnel. I was cold but drenched with sweat. A large barge was moored twenty yards from the end of the tunnel. I couldn't bring myself to walk past it. I thought of the boy's mother who'd fainted. There seemed to be somebody standing by the prow. My heart pounded. I moved forward. I said to myself, "There are no such things as ghosts." It was a bale or something. Another five yards and I'd be past it and in the open. Of course it was a bale, how could I have thought it could be anything else? The whistling and the footsteps behind had stopped. It was probably some kids having a joke. Then the bale moved. It *was* somebody. The bulky shadow moved towards me. I backed away. Because of the light behind I couldn't make out who or what it was. A match struck and flared. It made a terrific noise in the silence. The face looked terrible; orange and shadowy and it seemed to flicker.

"Well, well, well," said the voice. I gripped my cricket bat. It was Sawbridge. "Fancy us meeting like this."

I turned to run back up the tunnel. Two figures were standing there. They were Sawbridge's two pals, Skinner and Stelfox. I turned round. Sawbridge was moving towards me. He threw his cigarette butt into the water. It

hissed. I looked over my shoulder. There was no way out. They were almost upon me.

"Haven't got your little girlfriend with you tonight, have you?" hissed Sawbridge. The others laughed. "You can have a bit of fun with us instead."

"Could go swimming eh," said Skinner. Stelfox laughed. Sawbridge coughed and spat into the water.

"Nice night for it," he sneered.

The only way of escape was through the water to the opposite bank. As suddenly as I could I leapt on to the barge and scrambled across it, stumbling over packing cases and tarpaulins. I ran along its length, coughing and gasping. I could hear them shouting and crashing behind me. The far bank was about four yards off. It was awful jumping out into darkness. There wasn't much landing space either, maybe a couple of yards and I could easily crack my head on the curved roof. I clambered on to the upper level of the barge. I'd jumped diagonally in order to give myself as much landing space as possible. There was no time to think. I jumped with all my might, flinging the bat in front of me. My knees hit the crumbling pavement and I slipped back into the murky, evil-smelling water. The water closed over my waist. I stretched my hand and clasped a mooring rope. I dragged myself, panting and wet, up on to the bank. The three behind me wouldn't risk the leap. There was a splash beside me. Then another. They were throwing stones. Sawbridge had picked up a pole and was flailing at me. I pulled myself up until my face was level with the path. Two pinpricks of light stared into my face. An enormous rat. I felt something run across my neck and shoulder, then a splash. The rat had run across me and jumped into the water. I hauled myself on to dry land. Sawbridge was shouting, "I'll get you." I knew that if he caught me now he'd be even more mad because I'd got away.

I ran as fast as I could towards the light. My trousers were soaked. I knew that they'd make for the exit on the other side and climb over the tunnel to where I was. Whatever I did I had to be quick. My brain raced. Once out in the open, I looked desperately about me. I could see three shadowy figures racing for the light. I heard them scrambling over bushes and up on to the railway line that ran along the roof of the tunnel. On their side, in the distance, were the lights of houses and home. Somehow I had to get past them. On my side there was a lane lined by hedges and about thirty yards down on the left hand side a farm gate. If I could get there without them seeing me, I could hide, wait for them to rush past, then double back over the railway line. It was the only way. I sprinted down the lane as quickly as I could. I heard them shout, "There he goes," and they scrambled down the embankment. There was a slight bend that hid me from them. I dived down the small entrance overgrown with dandelions and dock leaves. The gate looked as though it had never been opened so I threw myself over, ran a few paces back towards my pursuers and crouched as deeply into the hedge as I could. A thorny branch scraped across my cheek and I felt blood trickle down my face. I didn't feel the pain.

I heard their footsteps approaching and heard their voices.

"Down here."

"I want him first," said Sawbridge.

"Me second, then," said Skinner. They both laughed. They weren't fooling. I knew Stelfox had beaten up a kid at their school so badly he'd had to go to hospital. I held my breath. They stopped so close to me I could see their legs through the hedge. Could almost touch them.

"Might have gone back."

"Naw."

"That turning by the dairy." They looked up the lane. I was willing them to go that way.

"Could be hiding here."

I couldn't move. I was trying not to breathe, trying to make my chest rise and fall as slowly as possible. I was longing to take a great gulp of air. If they found me, there was nowhere else to run. Just a wide empty field. A black and white cow munched at some grass. She didn't care that I was in trouble. I heard them moving towards the gate. They were coming for me. I closed my eyes.

Then Sawbridge said, "Come on," and I heard them

running away down the lane. I waited until I heard their footsteps disappearing, took a great gulp of air and crept out from my hiding place. I sneaked a look up the road. I could still see Skinner and Sawbridge. Stelfox must have already gone round past the dairy. They were far enough away for me to make a sprint for it. I ran as quickly as I could. There was a shout behind me and I heard their feet running. I was quite a fast runner and I knew they were too far behind to catch me unless I fell down or something. I wasn't worried. I was going to get away this time, I thought to myself, but I'd have to be extra careful in the future. I knew what they were like. Sawbridge would never forgive Skipper for what he'd done. Because I'd seen it happen, as far as he was concerned beating me up was almost as good. Anyway, for the time being, I was safe. I mounted the banking towards the railway line. When I got to the top I turned and looked back. I could see Skinner and Sawbridge running towards me. I wondered where Stelfox had got to. I gave a wave and turned to go. Two arms clutched. I looked up. Now I knew that Stelfox had stayed behind.

"Got you," he said.

I tried to struggle but he was as strong as a horse.

"Thought you'd get away did you? Thought you'd get away from Stelfox?"

Then he pushed me with all his might. I rolled headlong down the embankment. It knocked all the breath out of my body. When I looked up I saw the figures of Sawbridge and Skinner towering over me. Sawbridge clutched my lapels and hauled me to my feet. Stelfox came leaping down the embankment holding my bat, which I'd dropped when he pushed me. They stood round me

breathing and grinning. Then Sawbridge pushed me hard on to the ground. They pinned me down.

"Here," said Sawbridge, "this is my friend, Taters."

He struck me hard across the jaw with the back of his hand so that it made my teeth rattle. I could smell his tobacco breath.

"Haven't got your cripple friend to help you now."

"Good job for you," I shouted defiantly. I had nothing to lose. "He may be a cripple but he could beat you to a custard any day of the week."

Sawbridge didn't like that. It didn't sound good in front of his mates.

Smack. He struck me again. I felt a tooth come loose.

"Funny man, eh?" he snorted.

"What we gonna do with him?" asked Skinner.

Sawbridge thought for a minute. "I think," he said, "we ought to get him to say sorry for being so very, very rude to me."

I don't mind saying I'm sorry, I thought, as long as I can get away.

"Listen, Tatermash." He pulled at my shirt until I was on my feet. I heard my shirt tear. "Listen. I want you to say, 'Sorry Mr Sawbridge for all the bad things I said about you and I promise never to say them again.'"

I'd changed my mind. "No," I said.

"Say it," he said, flicking me across the nose so that it bled. "Say it or you won't be able to walk home."

I swallowed. "Sorry Sawbridge . . ."

"Mr Sawbridge."

"Sorry, Mr Sawbridge, for all the bad things I said about you and I promise . . ."

"Never to say them again."

"Never to say them again."

Sawbridge didn't look satisfied. I could taste the blood in my mouth.

"I don't think he meant it," he said to his pals. He turned to me with an almost sad look on his face. "I don't think you meant what you said. Unless you mean it I'm going to have to give you a doing-over."

"I should do him over anyway," said Stelfox. He was the one who really frightened me. There was something mad about him. Mad and cold.

"Mean it!" screamed Sawbridge pulling me right up to him. "I want to hear it from the heart. From the heart, sonny. Understand?"

I understood and repeated the sentence.

He seemed satisfied this time. He nodded, then smiled. "Now we're going to beat you up anyway."

Stelfox smiled at this. The thought of beating somebody about always cheered him up. He picked up my cricket bat. Ran his hand across the blade thoughtfully. "It would be fitting justice, sportsman," he said to me, "if, after running away from us and being so rude and nasty to brother Sawbridge here, you was not to play cricket any more."

I wasn't quite sure what he meant but it scared me.

"You like to play cricket," said Stelfox.

"He's a sportsman," said Skinner.

"A sportsman," agreed Stelfox.

I felt the other two wouldn't go as far as him but they didn't want to stop him. I decided to try and humour him.

"Yes, I like playing cricket," I said. I knew that I mustn't sound frightened. It would only encourage them. What they wanted more than anything was for me to be frightened. In a flash I saw my mum sewing in front of the fire and my dad doing his crossword. I'd have given anything to be safe back home. If only someone would come past, I thought.

"There you are," said Stelfox, "I knew he was a sportsman. Here, sportsman, which hand d'you bat?" He hammered the bat hard into the ground next to my ear.

"Right hand," I said, "I bat right hand." I didn't know where this was leading.

"This one is it?" he said, half smiling, and he lifted up my right hand with the end of the bat.

"Yes," I said.

He tapped my wrist gently with the bat then harder and harder. "What a pity it would be if this hand was to be broken in an accident, wouldn't it, sportsman?"

I couldn't answer. Even Stelfox wouldn't do that, I thought.

"WOULDN'T IT, SPORTSMAN?" he screamed, his face going red.

"Yes," I said, nearly crying. I was really frightened now.

"Of course, sportsman, being an accident you'd have to tell people as how it was an accident otherwise, sportsman, you might find you had another accident to your left hand."

"Please don't," I cried, "please."

There was no way out of this. I knew he was capable of breaking my hand. The others wouldn't stop him in case they were accused of being soft. I didn't think even Sawbridge wanted to go that far. He could see trouble looming the next day, maybe trouble with the police. All Stelfox could see was my hand, the bat and a sort of pleasure. I could see that Sawbridge was a bit worried.

"Stretch it out," said Stelfox.

"Here," said Sawbridge, trying to interrupt.

"Stretch it out," screamed Stelfox. Then, just as suddenly, he was calm again. He smiled. He could see the bat coming down. See my hand breaking up. It made him really happy.

I struggled to keep my hand away but they fell on me and Sawbridge pinned my right arm with the palm of my hand to the ground.

"Unless he's got something to say," said Sawbridge.

Although I was frightened my brain was working fast. I knew somehow that if I could give Sawbridge something, something that really cost me, he'd accept it instead of the beating. It was like one of those bargains I was always making with myself. Sawbridge turned my hand over and spread the fingers on a flat piece of plank. Stelfox was swinging the bat in large circles. It was as though smashing hands was a kind of art.

"You ain't got your hero here now," said Sawbridge.

Then I saw what he wanted and what I had to give him. They were both holding my hand now. Stelfox lowered the bat slowly in a big arc so that it touched the back of my wrist. He was like a golfer taking a practice swing. He lifted the bat.

"Wait!" I screamed.

They paused. The bat hung in the air. Even Stelfox must have sensed the urgency in my voice.

"What?" asked Sawbridge.

I licked my lips. I hated what I was going to do and I wasn't even sure it was going to work. "My pal," I said. "Skipper. It's all lies. What he said about his dad and the War. It's all lies."

It was all out. Even as I told the truth, as it came tumbling out, the story I'd promised Skipper and his

117

mum that I'd never repeat, even as I told it I knew that I had to make it seem that it cost me. It wasn't difficult to cry. I even managed to tell them that I'd promised never to tell it. If I was to get away I knew they had to believe that what I was saying cost me as much pain as a broken hand. If they didn't believe that it was all over.

When I'd finished, Sawbridge stood up. They let my hand go. I lay on the grass sobbing hysterically. Great gasping sobs. Half of it was regret.

"All right," said Sawbridge.

Already I wished I'd had my hand broken rather than betray Skipper. But it was too late. It was done now.

Stelfox was disappointed. He had been looking forward to breaking me up.

"Ain't we gonna crack him?" he asked. He moved forward. Sawbridge stopped. Sawbridge was a big lad. Even Stelfox wouldn't cross him unless he had to.

"Leave him," said Sawbridge.

Stelfox threw the bat away in disgust. Sawbridge clutched me by the shirt collar with both hands and pulled me up.

"Listen, Tatermash," he hissed, "You keep out of my way see? Understand? And when you see me, be very polite indeed."

I nodded.

"Now if I see your little mate, I'm gonna have to tell him what you said. Tell him the whole story."

"No," I said, "You mustn't."

Sawbridge laughed. "The whole story," he repeated then all my breath left my body in one gush as his fist thumped into my stomach. Then Stelfox kneed both my arms so that I couldn't feel them. He stood back with his feet apart while Skinner punched me across the temple

118

and kneed my stomach. I lay on the ground groaning, trying to force some breath into my lungs but it wouldn't go.

The three moved off down the embankment. They were finished with me.

I don't know how long I lay there. I ached all over. But I didn't really feel it. A word kept going through my head. I could see Skipper in his chair as he'd been when we first met. He was smiling at me. And the word kept pounding in my brain. Judas, it said. Judas. A train whistled as it rattled past above my head. I thought of all those strangers on the train. How lucky they all were. None of them had just betrayed his best friend. The train whistled again. Then its lights disappeared into the dusk. I watched the place where it had been. Far off in the distance, and faintly now, it whistled again.

I pulled myself to my feet, picked up my bat and stumbled home through the gathering gloom.

Chapter Eight

As the days passed and the final with Yorkshire got closer, I knew there was something I had to do. I had to tell Skipper what had happened between me and Sawbridge; had to tell him that I'd told him about Skipper's dad. I had no idea how I was going to go about it but I just knew it had to be done. I remembered how Mrs Skipton had once said that she'd always tell me the truth. That's what I'd have to do with Skipper. Not dress it up at all or make any excuses but tell it exactly as it had been, make my part sound as bad as it was. What was most important was that he should hear it from me first. Whatever row we'd had before I was sure that if Sawbridge happened to see him and tell him first, our friendship would be over. A number of times I set out through our front gate intending to go to his house and tell him the whole story straight out. That would be the best way, I thought. He'd open the door and before he had time to even say "Hello" or anything I'd say, "Skip, I've told somebody about your dad." I'd even worked out a little speech and learned it by heart. Four or five times I set out, repeating my speech, but when I got to the end of our Avenue my courage ran out and I had to turn back. How ashamed Skipper would have been of me. Twice I even got to his front door. I walked up to it like a machine man just putting one foot in front of the other, not thinking, dead mechanical. Then I was at the door. I looked at it. It seemed much bigger than I remembered. I lifted my hand to ring the bell. But I couldn't do it. I walked down the path telling myself what a coward I was. Stopped, went back and tried again. Lifted my hand. But I still couldn't do it. I walked home looking at the cracks in the pavement. The day of the final was fast approaching. I had to tell him before then. Suppose he turned up at the game and I still hadn't told him. Suppose Sawbridge was there; I knew it was unlikely but suppose he was and he saw Skipper and went over and told him so that everybody could hear. I could just see Sawbridge's face, all twisted up, combing his hair. "Hello," he'd say in that way of his, "your mate, Tater-mash, told me something really interesting about your dad. You know, the hero . . ." It would be terrible if that happened.

On the afternoon before the game I made up my mind that whatever happened, I would tell him. I rehearsed my little speech to the mirror and set off. I kept giving myself milestones. Little landmarks. The end of the Avenue; the patch of empty ground near Seagers Lane; the lamp post where Melrose Avenue turned into his street. I even made myself pretend that I was on my way somewhere I really wanted to go. "Just going to the library," I said to myself. But inside, my heart was sinking and an awful fear gripped me. There was no fooling myself. I knew what I had to do. Their green front gate was closed. I took a deep breath; had a last practice. "Oh hello Skipper," I said aloud to myself, "before you say anything, there's something I have to tell you."

I pushed open the gate and walked up the path. The gravel crunched under my feet. I tried to walk as quietly

121

as possible. It was funny but I didn't want him to hear me and come spinning full pelt round the corner of the house in his chair. That's how I'd seen it. If he didn't come to the door as I'd imagined it I knew I wouldn't be able to say what I had to say. So I walked as quietly as I could. If Mrs Skipton came to the door I had a plan for that too. I wouldn't go in when she invited me. Wouldn't let her start talking. I'd say very quietly but firmly, "Can I speak to Skipper please?"

I was at their front door. I tried to lift my hand. But it wouldn't move. "Come on Taters," I said to myself. Then, without thinking, I ignored the bell and found my fist hammering on the door as if the house was on fire. I stood back from it. I could hardly breathe. I listened for footsteps. The squeak of Skipper's chair. But there was nothing. I rang the bell. It echoed in the silence.

I walked away from the house. I felt a bit better. I'd tried, hadn't I? I could always say to Skipper now, "Skipper, I tried to tell you. Came round, knocked on the door, rang the bell and everything but there was no answer." But deep inside me I knew it wasn't right. I was only protecting myself. I thought I might try again the next morning but there wouldn't be time. I hoped maybe he'd turn up at the game and I'd be able to tell him then. Just as strongly I hoped that Sawbridge wouldn't get there first. I couldn't bear to think about that.

At the town ground we changed in the big pavilion. It smelled of dust and wood. On the walls were photographs of teams going back to about 1905. Skipper would have loved it. There were more than two hundred people in the ground and they all clapped when we went out to field. It was a bright day but not really warm. The County flag fluttered from the top corner of the pavilion

122

and two or three seagulls pecked at the grass near where I was fielding on the boundary. When the ball came out towards me they flew up in the air crying but soon came down again. Yorkshire Schoolboys made one hundred and thirty-four. I even got a bowl but didn't take any wickets. At half-past twelve we went into the pavilion. There was salad with ham and we drank lemonade and orange juice. By three o'clock we went in to bat and managed to make ninety very slowly. I made four but I was run out so it didn't look as bad as if I'd been bowled. All the time we were batting I kept looking out for Skipper. But there was no sign of him.

The next day, Saturday, Yorkshire went in again. They had some really stylish players. Their first wicket down was a kid called Hemming. He batted with his shirt sleeves buttoned down and scored thirty-eight all along the ground. You felt he could have scored sixes if he'd wanted to but that he felt it was wrong to hit the ball in the air. He just had the look of a real cricketer. When he hit the ball, even though it was just a defensive stroke, he followed right through. He had real style. After lunch Yorkshire declared. Hemming was still batting. He struck the ball through the covers for four, turned to the umpire and said, "Declaration, Umpire," and walked off towards the pavilion peeling off his gloves. I couldn't wait until I was made captain and could declare in the same way.

We were left with one hundred and twenty-one to draw and one hundred and twenty-two to win. We started badly and lost our three best players for twenty. Geoff Poole, our captain, got hit in the face, broke his glasses and had to go to hospital. It wasn't going well for us. When I got to the wicket I didn't seem to be able to concentrate properly. For about four overs I kept missing the ball or getting little edges that didn't quite go for catches. I'd been in about a quarter of an hour and had made five lucky runs when they brought back this fast bowler called Harnden who had taken two wickets already. His first ball was a bit short outside the off stump. The cover drive was my favourite stroke. I swept my bat forward but the ball just caught the edge. It flew high into the air, too high to be a slip catch, bounced a couple of times before crossing the boundary for a lucky four. The spectators clapped. They knew it wasn't a good stroke but they wanted to encourage me. As a kind of joke I waved my bat in the air, like you do when you've scored fifty. And there was Skipper in his chair. I waved again to show I'd seen him. He lifted up his left arm and swung it forward. I knew what he meant by that. Straight bat. The next ball came across my body to the left side. I turned my bat and glanced it down past leg slip. We ran three. Suddenly I was getting the feel of the ball again. The bat, instead of being something clumsy that was separate from me, felt like an extension of my arm. I didn't have to hit hard but strike through the ball in the direction I wanted to go. I wondered whether I ought to roll my sleeves down and button them like I'd seen Hemming do. I decided not to bother. If I couldn't bat in my own style what was the point? I could see Mrs Skipton wheeling Skipper round the boundary until they were near the sight screen. Skipper had probably asked her to do that so that he could see better what the ball was doing through the air and off the pitch. She walked back to the pavilion leaving Skip on his own. My mum and dad were sitting on two deck chairs that they'd brought with them. I could see Dad pouring tea into a cup from his thermos flask. Mum was reading *Home Chat*. Skipper didn't move. His eyes were on the play all the time. He didn't miss anything. If I could manage to make a decent score, over fifty, I bargained, I'd go over to Skip and tell him the whole story. I wouldn't even bother to go to the pavilion to take my pads off. Just walk straight out to where Skipper was to tell him. After I'd promised myself that, none of it seemed so difficult. The fact that Skipper had come meant that he'd forgiven me for what had happened. I felt a kind of electricity going through me. The sort of feeling you get when you're climbing up a tree or a cliff and look down suddenly. You get a feeling you can do anything. I was going well. Already I'd made twenty-nine. One pull shot I played off a short ball even Hemming applauded. I thought, maybe he'll start rolling his sleeves up in order to look like me. Of course he didn't.

The next shot I got a single. When I turned round at the other end a knife went through my heart. Along the boundary, walking towards where Skipper was sitting, were three figures. It was Sawbridge and his two mates. I prayed that somehow they wouldn't see Skipper. If only his mother had been there they might have walked by. I thought of running over there and then trying to tell him before they said anything but already the bowler was running in. I didn't even see that ball. Hardly played a stroke. Somehow it missed the wicket. The three of them were standing near Skipper's chair. I could see him looking up. It was terrible not being able to do anything. I don't know how I managed to carry on batting. I even scored a four. Sawbridge was leaning to one side looking the other way. I started laying about me with the bat. In a way I was almost trying to get myself out but luck seemed to be on my side. I didn't seem able to miss. Soon I got fifty. I waved to the crowd. I saw my dad explaining to Mum and she began to clap. All this time I was wondering what Sawbridge was saying to Skip and how he was feeling. Then, they were gone. I'd run three for a stroke past long leg and when I came back they weren't there any more. Skip was slumped in his chair, his head down. He was wheeling his chair backwards and forwards. Just a couple of feet each way; backwards and forwards; backwards and forwards over and over again. The next ball I put all I felt about Sawbridge into it. The ball flew high, high into the air, dropping just short of the boundary and into the hands of Hemming. I was out. I ran from the wicket. As I went through the gate Hemming said quietly, "Well done." I tore off my pads and gloves as quickly as I could and ran round the boundary to where Skip was sitting. He was wheeling himself away.

"Skipper," I shouted.

He just kept on going. He was travelling really fast. His arms going like pistons. I could tell he didn't care where he went. I shouted again. I heard a woman say to her husband, "Wasn't that the lad who made those runs?" I had to run to catch up with the chair. I ran past and stood in front of him with my legs apart blocking his path. He just kept on coming, wheeling his chair until it cannoned off my legs. In a funny way I was glad it hurt. Skipper looked straight past me, as if I wasn't there.

"Get out," he said, "get out of my way."

"About Sawbridge," I started to explain but he wouldn't listen. The cold look in his eye stopped me. I thought, it would be terrible to have Skipper as an enemy. I could see he'd been crying. His eyes were all red and swollen but I knew he would never cry in front of me. He looked up.

126

"Why?" he said. "Why?"

"They would have beaten me up," I said. It sounded tame.

Skipper spat out two words. "So what," he answered. "So what." He wasn't angry. He was cold. Cold as ice. "You had to tell, didn't you?"

"I'm sorry," I said. It sounded so feeble.

"You. You had to tell, didn't you? I thought we were friends." He spat it out sarcastically, "Friends!" We looked at one another. "I thought we were friends," he said again. And then added with a voice like a whip, "But I was wrong, wasn't I?" And he wheeled round and past me towards the road. I could have followed but I knew it was hopeless. Mrs Skipton was standing by her car which was parked on some grass. She waved to me. Out of habit I waved back. Skipper's words rang in my ears. There was applause from the crowd. Yorkshire had been beaten. The players streamed towards the pavilion. People were standing up. I bet my dad would be explaining to Mum what had happened and she would stand up and clap so as not to be different. But none of this meant anything to me; all I could hear was Skipper's voice over and over again in my ears.

"I thought we were friends but I was wrong, wasn't I?"

"No," I said, then shouted out loud, "No."

I had a feeling that we would never see each other again. The feeling wouldn't go away. Slowly I walked towards the pavilion. I saw the Humber gliding away. Our coach patted me on the back as I climbed the pavilion steps.

"Well played, Tattershall," he said.

"Thanks," I said, "thanks very much."

Chapter Nine

After that I didn't even try to go round to see him. But he was still in my mind. I kept thinking of ways in which we could make it up. Because we'd beaten Yorkshire in the final we went on a tour of Devon and Cornwall for two and a half weeks so I didn't really have a chance to see him. I really enjoyed the tour. We stayed with different families everywhere we went and travelled around in a charabanc. It also meant that I was able to miss school. It was dead good travelling down country lanes singing songs and thinking of all the other kids back at school doing arithmetic or history.

When I got home again there was a parcel from Skipper waiting for me. I took it up to my bedroom to open it. Inside was the wooden figure of Larwood. He had been glued together very carefully so nobody would ever have known he'd been broken. On the underneath was written:

Harold Larwood
The bowler

The "the" was underlined. Skipper worshipped Larwood. In a separate envelope were the score books we'd used throughout the summer. Some of the pages were stained with orange juice but every ball, run, leg-bye and wicket was recorded in Skipper's neat pencil. The final Test was, of course, unfinished. I wondered why he had sent it. Was he forgiving me?

That afternoon I went over to his house to see him. It didn't seem difficult any more. I took the Wisden that he'd loaned me weeks ago. When I came out of the wood and on to the slope above the lawn there was nobody in the garden. The grass on the pitch had grown longer; too long to play on. Where the white lines had been and round the boundary the grass was a lighter green. All the players had been packed away along with the bats, the wickets, the score-board and cigar-tin wicket keeper. There was nothing left to remind you that four great contests had been fought out on that strip of ground over the summer. Three magpies stalked about in front of the house. I found myself reciting as I walked across to the back door, "One for sorrow, two for joy, three for a girl . . ." Near the boundary I felt something round and hard under my foot. I bent down. It was the marble. I slipped it into my pocket. Two of the magpies flew up into the air and over the house.

All the windows of the house were closed and the curtains drawn. I walked round to the front and rang the bell. Nobody came to answer it. I sneaked a look between the living-room curtains. I couldn't see anybody. There were sheets on all the furniture and all the books had been taken away. Without expecting an answer I walked round the outside of the house calling for Skipper's dog. Silence. A woman came out of the house next door. She had a bucket with a mop in it. When she saw me she came over, drying her hands on her pinny.

"You looking for somebody?" she asked.

"Have they gone away?"

"Yes they've gone away." She looked at me suspiciously. "You supposed to be there?"

"He's my friend," I said, "Skipper's my best friend." I felt good saying that. I didn't care if she thought it was stupid. The woman took a strand of grey hair and tucked it round the back into place with a hairpin she took from between her teeth.

"You never know these days," she said.

"Where have they gone. D'you know please?"

"Oh they left weeks ago. An ambulance came round. Then a van came for some of the furniture."

An ambulance. My heart sank. I hoped they hadn't gone far. I had to speak to Skip. I couldn't leave everything as it was.

"Where did they take him?"

"How should I know?"

I didn't have time to be polite.

"Come on. Try and remember." Then I added, "It's very important."

"Jerry did tell me. Wait a minute. They left an address in case anything should come through the post. I'll get it."

She went back into the house and came out again with a piece of paper in her hand.

"Here it is," she said. She took a pair of spectacles out of a pocket in her pinny and put them on. "I knew I had it somewhere." She held the paper up.

"Yes, here it is," she said. "It's the Cottage Hospital . . ."

I snatched the paper out of her hand and ran off down the drive.

"Here just a minute," shouted the lady. "Well I never." I didn't look back.

The Cottage Hospital where they were keeping Skip

130

was nearly three miles away. I felt in my pocket. Four-pence. Enough to get me there. Getting back didn't matter. It took hours for the bus to come. It always does whenever you are in a hurry. The bus stop was just outside the village laundry. You could smell the clothes and the damp even out in the road. At last the cream and red bus arrived. The hospital was in the middle of the country about half a mile down a lane. Some of the rooms were open and you could see people in pyjamas sitting up in bed reading magazines and books or just sleeping. An ambulance passed me but he didn't stop to offer me a lift. I thought, I should have limped. There was a big entrance hall and at the back a big desk. The lady behind it couldn't understand what I wanted. She looked through a book for Skipper's name. I remembered of course that his name was Skipton.

"There's a Malcolm Skipton," she said looking at me over the top of her specs. "Is that who you want?"

It sounded funny her saying Skipper's name and not knowing anything about him. I bet she'd never heard of Harold Larwood.

Skipper was in a ward called Sir Humphrey Stanley.

"Speak to the Sister first," said the lady.

It was up a staircase and you had to follow the signs. There was a funny smell everywhere and people wearing dressing-gowns. When I got to the ward they were serving dinner. The small, red-haired Sister was ticking things off on a piece of paper.

"And Mr Henry is 'diet'," she said.

She kept on ticking things off and shouting instructions all the time I was asking her about Skip. This time I called him Malcolm Skipton. I thought they might take me more seriously.

131

"Well, it's dinner time now," said the Sister. Then she must have seen my face. "Just for a few minutes, then."

Skipper was in a room on his own. Mrs Skipton was sitting on an easy chair near his bed reading a magazine. There weren't any flowers or anything. Skipper was asleep. She didn't seem surprised to see me. If she knew about me and Skip she didn't show it. She seemed pleased to see me but her eyes were tired. "He's asleep," she said.

I said, "I wanted to bring him the book he lent me." Then I thought that was the wrong thing to say because it might look as though I was returning the Wisden so that we could finish everything off. Mrs Skipton didn't seem to notice.

"I would have come before," I said, "but . . ." I shrugged.

"That's all right," she said. She gave me the book back. "Why don't you give it to him? He may wake up any minute. You sit with him for a bit. He'll be pleased to see you."

"Yes," I said.

"I'd hoped his father might have . . ." She broke off. She stood up. "You sit with him." She picked up her magazine and handbag and went out of the door quietly. She gave me a smile before she closed it. Even though she smiled, I could tell she was unhappy. It made me feel funny to think that a grown-up could be like that. It made me think that grown-ups weren't different people. It frightened me a bit. When she opened the door I heard the noise of the ward outside, then it went quiet again.

I looked at Skipper. He was sleeping peacefully. He looked a lot better than the last time I'd seen him. I knew though that some days he could be fit and strong, almost normal. Like he'd been that day we went on the beach and he drove the car or when he arm-wrestled with Sawbridge. Then the next day he would be an invalid again. It was funny to watch him sleeping. Not knowing I was there. Perhaps he was dreaming something; seeing all kinds of things that I couldn't. The windows were open and the curtains drifted in the breeze. I thought, what if he doesn't wake up and Mrs Skipton comes back. I'll miss my chance of telling him. I went to the door and opened it quietly. There was no sign of her. I thought I heard the sheets moving. I went back to the bed. Skipper was still fast asleep. Then, I said it. I know it sounds funny but I told him everything while he was asleep. All about his mother telling me about his dad. About me going to his house and not having the courage to ring his bell. About knocking on his door and no one answering. About how I'd been caught by Sawbridge by the canal and that I'd told him everything because otherwise they would have broken my hand. About wanting to tell him everything before the final because I didn't want him to hear it from anyone else first. The whole story just came pouring out. Most of the time I was talking I wasn't even looking at him. I had my hands knotted together and was looking at the floor. It all came out in a rush like a waterfall. I hardly took a breath. When I'd finished I just sat there still and silent. Just sat there looking at the floor. There was a rustling noise. At first I couldn't work out what it was. Then I looked to the bottom of the bed. The sheets were moving. Suddenly Skipper's foot popped up. His toes wriggled. I looked up to the head of the bed. He had one eye open, and he was smiling that smile of his.

"Toenails," he whispered.

"Toenails," I repeated.

133

His hand came out and gripped my arm. It didn't seem to be strong any more.

"I thought you were asleep," I said.

"Ah," he said as though he was a wise old owl. He sat up in bed. "Very good speech," he said.

He'd been awake all the time. I wasn't mad though. I was glad. Really glad. We didn't talk about it any more. It just didn't seem important. He seemed really pleased to see me. We talked like in the old days about the games, the names, the trips to the beach. It was like we'd never broken up.

"Pity we never finished the Series," I said.

"We have some good days in October," he said.

"Yes, good days," I said.

"England would have won anyway."

"With Larwood back."

There was a silence but it wasn't the kind of embarrassing silence you sometimes get. I was seeing the pitch and all the players set out in the sun. How the field was overgrown and they'd be living somewhere else when Skip got better.

"We might go back. And anyway there are other gardens. What's wrong with next summer?"

"Yes, next summer," I said. I thought about the hole that Sawbridge had dug.

"About Sawbridge," I began.

He wouldn't let me finish.

"People like him," he said, "they're a waste of good skin." It was one of his favourite phrases about people he didn't like. He looked up at me. "All you can do is try to make up for people like him. Honour's the thing."

I suddenly felt how much older he was than me. As if he'd been through two lifetimes already.

"Here," he said. "Got something for you." He turned over and reached into a drawer in his bedside table and took out the clasp knife. He opened my palm and placed it in it.

"Don't you want it?" I asked. I'd always liked that knife.

"Can't use it here," he said.

"What about after?"

He turned the knife over. Pointed to the handle.

"My dad's initials," he said.

I reached into my trouser pocket. "Got something for you." I took out the marble and put it in his hand. He looked at it closely for a long time as though he could see something in it. Then he closed his hand on it tightly.

"Oh," I said, remembering the book, "I nearly forgot." I handed him the Wisden. "You lent it to me."

He took it from me and turned over the pages until he found the record of the 1932–33 series.

"Nineteen thirty-two-thirty-three," he said.

"Sutcliffe." He smiled.

"Walter Hammond," I said.

"Ponsford."

"Richardson."

"Douglas Jardine."

"Oldfield."

"Don Bradman."

"Stan McCabe."

"Woodfull."

"Kippax."

"O'Reilly."

"Clarrie Grimett."

"Hedley Verity."

"Harold Larwood."

"Harold Larwood," he repeated.

"L.E.G. Ames," I said.

There was a silence. It was his turn. His eyes had closed. I took the book carefully from his hands.

"Voce, Allen, Bowes, Paynter." I stopped. He murmured drowsily.

"Larwood. There'll never be another like him."

It was as though he was talking in his sleep.

I hadn't heard Mrs Skipton come in. I stood up.

"Everything all right?" she asked.

"Fine," I said. Skipper was fast asleep. I put the book on the bedside table. Mrs Skipton gave me the bus fare home.

The next morning there was a letter waiting for me. It was an invitation to take part in winter nets with the England Schoolboy squad. All the way to the hospital on the bus I was thinking how excited Skipper would be at the news. I'd let him keep the letter. At the reception desk I heard the woman with glasses saying to somebody that visiting hours weren't for another two hours so I just sneaked by. I didn't really care. I was in enough trouble already because I should have gone back to school that day but I thought, what's the point of school if you're going to play cricket all your life? I could see myself walking out to bat in places like Somerset and Kent. Men in hats smoking pipes and reading newspapers applauding me all the way to the wicket in the early morning. "Isn't that the Tattershall who made that hundred against Australia?"

I dodged into a doorway when I saw the Sister coming. When the coast was clear, I tiptoed down to Skipper's room. I opened the door quietly. There was an old man sitting up in bed. He was drinking through a metal straw and there was a tube going into his arm from a bottle on a stand. I was in the wrong room. Skipper would laugh at that. I went out and crept to the room next door. No that wasn't it. I'd been right the first time. I couldn't understand. They must have moved him.

A nurse said, "What are you doing here?"

I told her. "I'm looking for Malcolm Skipton." It sounded funny to give his proper name.

"M. Skipton," she said, "M. Skipton. Didn't you know he died last night?"

A doctor hurried by, his white coat flapping. There was a stethoscope in his pocket. An orderly pushed a tray of bottles past. They clinked as they rolled. The nurse's face changed.

"Were you family or just a friend?" she asked.

I looked up at her. I couldn't make out her face very clearly. I wondered if I was going to faint.

"He was my friend all right," I said, "he was my friend."

Then I turned and rushed out of there, running as fast as I could down corridors and stairs. People called out to me but I didn't stop.

On the bus going home I just couldn't fit it all in. I couldn't make sense of what it meant to be dead. Where could all that life that Skipper had have gone to? I thought, if I go to the garden, he'll be there. I kept seeing his face as it had been that day in the rain, reflected in the glass. How it had looked like a ghost's. And I thought, that's what he is now. He's somewhere there, in that window. Then I remembered him saying that time we'd played Monopoly and he'd beaten me, "You'll be able to play plenty of times."

137

And I suddenly understood what he meant. I understood why he lived the way he did. He must have known. All that time he must have known.

That night I couldn't sleep at all. My mum asked me if I was all right but I couldn't tell her anything. I went to his house. I don't know why. I just wanted to be there. I didn't want to see anybody or talk to anybody. Even though it was autumn the sun was shining. Already some yellow leaves were falling. It would have been just the day to finish that final Test. Skipper would have hated leaving anything unfinished. I stood for a long time looking at the pitch. I somehow knew that I'd never come back to this place. That it was over. I wanted to leave something. I put my hands in my pocket and turned round. My fingers touched something cold and heavy. The knife. I took it out and unclasped the curved blade. It shone in the sunlight. I knew what I wanted to do. I walked to the tree that Skipper had climbed that day and started to carve on it. I did the best letters I could. It took me nearly an hour. When I'd finished I stepped back. It was good work. It said:

M. SKIPTON

And then in brackets:

(SKIPPER)

Underneath were two dates: 1936 then a dash and 1947. Below that I put just one word in large letters.

CRICKETER

I closed the knife and put it back in my pocket. Then I turned and walked out of that garden and never went back.

I didn't see Mrs Skipton or baby Sophie after that though I did get a letter from her about three weeks after Skipper had died. Reading her letter I thought we three would be the only ones who would really remember him. Then I started to think how the Skipper they would know couldn't really be the same Skipper that I would remember. That's how it was with everybody. Because of Skipper I was somehow different from how I had been before. He couldn't really be dead because some of him was in me too. It wasn't right that he should just disappear, and with him that hot and beautiful summer of 1947. So I thought I'd tell you all about him and then he'll be alive in you as well. Won't he?